Yuug Behuul

And The

Fountain

Of

Youth

An Exposé

Don. M. Denn

CALIFORNIA

For permission requests:
Contact publisher, addressed
"Attention: Permissions Coordinator,"
GENERAL PUBLISHING, Inc

Any references to historical events, real people, or real places
are used fictitiously. Names, characters, and places are
products of it's author's imagination.
Library of Congress Control Number: 1 2 3 4 5 6 7 8 9 10

Printed in America

Published by: GENERAL PUBLISHING, Inc.
CALIFORNIA

1

Fountain of Youth: Most High's Pod

Of everything there has ever been, every sort of useful life altering scientific thing humans have thus far managed to finagle out of nothingness, —bringing it into being out of his own ingenuity to make his own existence far easier, far more meaningful, ---still in existence everywhere one hoped it were available—a great many humans throughout earth have simultaneously raved about, as many a person's reached an incontrovertible consensus to be mind boggling, —-is Yuug Behuul's new contrivance joyfully christened: 'Most High's Fountain of Youth' he recently made accessible worldwide, a phenomenal consequence of a young child's labor---everyone was told, —a scientific derivative, —

citizens apprised from news was of some unknown technology—which when compared to every other man made thing, commanded—since it's unveiling to humanity, a fervor comparable in magnitude or attention only to Lemuel Gulliver's discovery of Lilliput.

"Dad, dad, look---"

"Yuggie, what is it?"

"Dad---its working, look what's on . . .!" Mr. Brask raised his bespectacled face he'd buried into his crumpled-up Los Angeles times

in his hands for long minutes---trying to make sense of whatever information was being broadcast in news bulletins, or what useful propaganda was currently circulating about what his son found so very exciting —-it required his immediate attention.

Sitting there pensive, he was mighty unsure of which media should hold more of his attention, till on some unknown prompts, his decision came to favor viewing rather than reading, then he sat there gazing intently at it's unnecessarily huge screen his son's incessant whining compelled him to buy recently—if not for him, for their home, deeply aware of what his son's outbursts signified.

Goings-on being telecast on his screen was of throngs of senior citizens, especially ones too concerned with eventually losing their finer bodily features due to passage of time, a prospect none of them found comforting, a queue constituted by elders afraid life's end was nigh, it represented their last ditch effort to preserve themselves back to youth in whatever way they could, were lined up. Their resolution not to let a good opportunity slip by considering aortas of truth it is said came with recent news about it, some thought, —following constant failures of every single promise ever offered humankind by cosmetic giants like; Avon, Glaxo-Smithcline, along with their other contemporaries too numerable to mention, —while selling them lotions, pomades, oint- ments, or placebo pills their claims suggested could conquer every ailment including; facial wrinkles, their sagging skins, their once upright bodies observers could only see drooping, —but here they were every one of them, after decades of patronage of those beautifully packaged medication formulated as ointments or pills with hopes one more jar of it, or another, or another one contained solutions to aging capable of finally making good on these age old promises by giant multinationals, to reinstate youth---knowing all along it couldn't be attained, ---still, it did was keep hopes alive. It was all there was—left of humans---really, hopes, dreams, nothing more.

Immersed thoroughly in each person's private thoughts---every patiently waiting elder or senior, they remained under inclement weather braving temperatures reaching scorching limits just to keep their position till their turn was next---some patiently, some---outwardly agitated, their wrinkles still intact, their skins saggier than ever before, their bent frames much lowered than than they'd ever known it---heralding an ever approaching end they hope to avoid by waiting in line for their turn to be transmogrified.

Thoroughly relishing a carpenters expert workmanship on seat crafting---regarding how soothing his back along with his nether regions felt on their 'gigerson' settee, an also pensive Yuug Behuul figuring he could apply a line he read from some glossy magazine---'Good House-keeping' he thought it was, ---into a conversation with his father sometime later - whether it made sense or not---where it said; 'it is *a generally accepted opinion following a shattering of unanimous trust by people on products humanity once trusted when incessant hyping's of badly coupled---sometimes unfinished ones from other lands arrived our shores through importation, turns to be, ---em---spoiler alert! ---just another hoax! ---so that general apathy becomes rife about town each time a new one is launched, but although, truth be told, at long last, things turned out just fine, people could only pucker up after adapting themselves to making do with bad products they were previously known to criticize vehemently, for its reduced qualities, to accept Yuggy's transmogrifier as what was worth it for them.*

Humanity least expected what it realized much later in retrospect, commanded ill founded fears then, or erroneously presumed to be one of those get rich quick schemes by it's proprietors---whoever they were, in their setting out to perform a service to mortals then, ---by gifting a much sought after solution to homosapien's most perturbing challenge, aging. Thankfully, for its genuineness, ---was without any fuss received wholeheartedly.

To some, news heralding Yuug Behuul's transmorgrifier gradually transcended their imagination---becoming real: a spellbinding new toy many called it at first, ---their term for amusement of any one interested in listening to gossip or news, but now, no one could use some rest once it was sighted on TV screens, it held people spellbound what a tall glistering dome looming in a certain Big Sur mansion somewhere in northern California, could possibly be.

In utter amazement, attendees stood motionless, eyes peeled, gazing upon a structure eighty-one feet high by twenty-seven feet in circumference—its owners were claimed at every opportunity, was constructed to undertake genetic repairs no known science before now could muster a solutions for.

A general consensus among scientists covertly present in Yuug Behuul's home, plus, heightening energy in representatives from corporate interests, kept Redwood agog with subdued activities that didn't seem like what could go away anytime soon especially now there was certitude something good was at hand, still, it was imperative they approached issues cautiously, wait to hear it's owner's account then determine what good information to deduce from any presumed facts

provided, after all, neither side: covert scientists—on one, nor potential corporate investors—on another, lacked any knowledge ——modern speed of scientific research often providential in answering pressing age related problems, sometimes led to disastrous outcomes. Notwithstanding, here today they all were in Big Sur mansion alongside people from all walks of life, many with careers irrelevant to Yuug Behuul's dome: media houses in persons of their journalists eager to report juicy piece of news of all time they presumed to catapult them into fame, police officers, government agents—ordered there to do a commanders bidding, international diplomats invited to witness it all, some were not. Then billionaires, theirs was a gumption compelling them to attend, since they might just find a good investment worthy of enterprise. Finally were covert spies including those from governments, corporate head quarters, all hoping they'd found what could ultimately transubstantiate into a career goldmine worth millions in valuable information comprising of a first hand proof of its existence to take home to master or boss or corporate executives under whose employ they were before any considerations could be put to practice. Regarding special government agents covertly present, their concerns included being present to read miranda rights to whomever owned it should any issues like hoaxers seeking to bamboozle societies of elderly folks or America at large with a phony sort of construction, ever arose, ——otherwise— their presence at their mansion was certain to help ensure security around a small child's monumental gizmo in exchange for good cash tips from his father.

They stood in small groups engrossed in conversations, some were at lost for what to do. Everyone stared in amazement at Yuug Behuul's sparkling glass dome correctly adjudging it too other--worldly by everyone of them to lend description to, it was too fearsome in its every essence---no one there neither knew what to make of it, nor call it. Too deeply engrossed, none noticed a little boy trod one step after another on a curvy staircase anticlockwise of where they stood marveling en route to coming towards them.

"It's called transmorgrifier, —with a T," everyone heard a small child's voice say momentarily distracting them from viewing his machine,

"It's called what---?" —a shrill female voice rang out clearly from where a group of seven journalist huddled together—away from other spectators.

"Transmorgrifier, it's going to make us young again, at least, it's what my dad says."

"Excuse me, you are who? —kid could you please identify yourself?"

"My name is Morsan Brask, Yuug Behuul too, I stank a lot when I didn't take my bath when I was young, they call such kids Yuug Behuul, it's what my mom said---, but I shower these days, mind you."

"Oh---ho! —when you were young, ey? —how old are you if I might ask?"

This commentators remarks to Yuug Behuul's response stirred some laughter from everyone there, it was apparent they all understood he hoped to bring himself down to Yuug Behuul's level with sassy language to be able to find out if he was really what was being spoken of as mankind's savior said to have---though they couldn't see how, created what could reverse aging. There were no reasons to doubt he was, —for here he was in Brask mansion where it all began—an only kid around gradually emerging a reliable spokesperson capable of providing needed information without guidance. For his comportment, he cast before their eyes a picture of one of those sensible children parents were want to be proud of in public places, he was but a small child of no more than ten—yet sensible, he had to be Yuug Behuul.

"Yuug Behuul you say? —Yuug Behuul they say built that over there?" inquired he nodding his head towards Yuug Behuul's dome where it stood, Yuug Behuul in turn nodded his head as well,

"Morsan Brask too, but I think I like Morsan Brask more, it makes me feel like I am no longer little, you know, almost as big as you folks."

Folks laughed some more.

"All right Morsan Brask---Yuug Behuul---whatever, do you know if your dad wants to sell it? --- You know, ---assuming it does what you say it does, I think you said you dad invented it."

Regardless of his immature age, Yuug Behuul could already tell folks were salivating over their transmorgrifier, it was also apparent to him they were wondering when one of such things could take its place by their side as an asset of theirs or a property.

Posing these questions compelled another to inquire as to his identity, and was informed it was Duran Buckler, a billionaire come to see Mr. Morsan Brask, or his young son Yuug Behuul.

Yuug Behuul's father regarded him closely concluding he couldn't be any younger than eighty-five early nineties at most---perhaps a little older, but not very, or perhaps, he was in his early nineties. His appearance or demeanor was of a rich fellow, richer in appearance than anyone he'd ever seen or met.

Answers provided by Yuugy had only deepened Duran Buckler's confusion, as it failed to remove any mystery of what it was capable of doing surrounding there, questions whose answers should explain it or its inner workings lingered: what composed? Could it in all actualities reverse age like hearsay touted it could, or, if according to certain enduring portions of gossip encompassing its emergence, suggesting all it could really do for one was repair wrinkles, fix age spots on one's skin, thereby making one feel young again, was true, ---he or she still remaining his or her age. In any case, during several of his thinking processes, his opinion in either case was a total support, with him being all for it---if it could make one younger again, then he'd call it wonderful, but if all it could do really was eliminate wrinkles on his skin making one look twenty years younger, it was also okay by him, though his previous position over it all favored smoothing out wrinkles to make people feel or look younger which he presumed was better anyhow as it would have resulted from reversing one's age

"You say someone called 'Most High' invented it then gave it to another called Gohabruhi-El, it was then brought down to you?"

"Yes sir, it was a long time ago when I was almost a baby, but I remember it well, it's what he told us, ---me, his name was, he was like thirty storey's tall---maybe even more---I can't remember, but it was awesome, I could never forget it even I tried to, Oh, oh---my dad also told me never to, he also said to everyone he invented it there being none willing to accept my story, or believe me if I told them a really tall man---geez!---he was really scary---while he approached, everything lying about leaped upwards, falling back down again each time his feet thudded earth's surface, but there was no earthquake---you know? ---like we usually have it here in California. Or maybe, it was his dad conveying it himself to us---just can't say, he bequeathed it to us himself, I think he later said it was a gift from his dad to us humans, he also said his father was no longer angry with us: we neither showed him any gratitude to him our creator, nor waited to be dismissed before running into Gohabruhi-El---he said our earth was called, to discover how beautiful it was for ourselves, ---without his permission."

"Your dad told you, but you don't really know or remember it clearly, do you?"

"No, I told you it's what my dad---. it was what really big man---, oh---well, forget about it, you wouldn't understand---"

"I see, where's your dad now?"

"He'll be down anytime soon."

Turning to everyone else numbering two dozen more than a hundred, Billionaire man Duran Buckler offered a suggestion,

"Transmorgrifier it is called, should it be what our little man here says it is, it is sure enough to die for, I wouldn't mind dying for being young again---"

They howled in laughter.

Elderly Duran Buckler continued speaking in a most wise manner characteristic of people of his age, some arguments he postulated momentarily earned him a lot of agreement from others,

"Nothing one wouldn't do to benefit from his machine if what he over there—" added he—gesturing towards Yuug Behuul standing by father, "—is saying were true."

"It's true, it's true, we've done it on some folks a while back, everyone of them is young again. One told my dad his' presently was a vitality similar to a twenty year old's. He showed us a photo of himself when he was young, then showed us another of his photos now he's young again,, it's true, he's young again. Another one we did on says he is now twenty-two years old, ---he goes about telling everyone how he felt he'd be propagating falsehood were he to tell others he was more than so. Mister McDougal was our third client, he says he could run faster than he could when he was nineteen, —nineteen being a long time ago---seventy years no less, twenty years again after he clocked seventy, if you ask me, I'd say he's young again---"

Following accounts of some of Yuug Behuul's family's associates had already benefiting from transmogrification, thoughts began to stray from; *'What a wonderful sight it was, but, was it really all it is made out to be? ---or were there necessary information being withheld from everyone'*, to, —*very interesting, or really, there had been successes already!*

There were murmurs of discontentment or of doubt, but in all, a secret sense of excitement held grip on almost everyone, there was nothing wrong with a second youth, but if obnoxiousness—which he came across as being, convinced him his childishness sufficed to save him impending multiple raps on his noggin—however sharp, however not so much so—were his statements to turn out to be a significant untruth, he had another thing coming or other issues to settle.

These dignitaries refrained from attempting to question Yuug Behuul deeper till his dad who'd retraced his steps back upstairs showed up, over enthusiasm, —if it couldn't be stifled, might yet cost any real progress made, none cared about counting chickens before eggs hatched, only to find snakes, roaches were all raised.

When after a long minute silence continued to reign, Duran Buckler---comported better than most there spoke,

"Your dad---young Mr. Brask: Yuug Behuul you say your name is---"

"Yes sir, Yuug Behuul,"

"When'll he be down?"

Young Mr. Brask: Yuug Behuul, was about offering Mr Buckler an honest answer when footsteps approached. Looking up, they saw men arrive second floor's landing to begin descending step after step to bring themselves towards where everyone awaited.

"Oh, there's my dad, those are some of them, ---I told you; my dad, his two assistants: subjects successfully initially put through transmogrification."

With silent curiosity continuing to hold a good grip on them all, whilst inquisitiveness hovering since their arrival now assuming companionship with their minds almost to comparable extents —but was now compelling them forward—-towards Mr. Brask's six approaching individuals with questions ready to be tossed at them. Everyone spoke simultaneously, noise, noise, inglorious noise was everywhere, a certain palpable sense of exhilaration lending itself them noticeably overtook their emotions. —Here was an opportunity to find out hidden truths surrounding Yuug Behuul's crystal or quartz transmorgrifier rising eight storey high.

Numbering seven, —they came across as fellows—bonds of friendship held too fast for anyone to separate, obviously induced by renewed youth or handsome cash payments, were chattering amongst themselves too satisfied to care about anything apart from bringing themselves down before TV cameras primed to sail their images to an ocean of eyes in homes everywhere---subsequent events proved to them—hadn't any intentions of treating them well: not least a disdain-fulness awaiting humans already commenced expressing at them should their claims of discovering of what was essentially, 'a fountain of youth', in big Sur California turn out to be anything less than what utterly satisfies planet earth's curiosity. But in truth, these were business part-ners: one, a proprietor of a new enterprise, others, his subjects.

BEFORE
James Clunky 108 yrs old

AFTER
James Clunky 108 yrs young

Stopping before media impatience could take them apart, they tried comporting themselves properly for interviews to commence. Senior older Mr. Brask took his place behind CNN's microphone while his test subjects flanked him on both sides, seeing this, Yuggy immediately switched sides from his home's visitors to where his father stood.

Walking away from where he stood conversing with Duran Buckler, Yuug Behuul headed to stand beside his father: Mr. Brask, a man in his late forties---by rudely squeezing himself past some of their test subjects signed into contract flanking him on both sides, then frantically apologizing to them for his bad behavior.

To his immediate left was one---observers later suggested couldn't have been a day beyond twenty-two, but was no less than ninety nine.

For Mr. Buckler whom championing a cause for finding facts continually became an issue of utter concern but was now subjected to waiting patiently, he realized he needed to continue leading if his goals were to remotely have a chance at success, of everyone there, only he arrived there with some noteworthy intentions.

"You are going to command 'many thanks' from everyone out there if your device turns out to be true Mr. Brask, is it?"

Mr. Brask made to offer his answer to elderly Duran Buckler, but was interrupted,

"These young fellows with you Mr. Brask, are they your employees Mr. Brask?"

"Yes, but also no," Yuug Behuul's father began saying, but his response appeared unacceptable to his visitors each one bent on finding out every truth as it were.

Paraphernalia on a sizeable number of fellows in Yuug Behuul's great room indicated nearly every one---if not all, were not just journalists who wouldn't quit no matter what, but ones from reputable media organizations across America evidently instructed---from their apparent readiness, to not settle for anything less than facts---if considering people's usual opinion of: *'uncertainties was what really accounted for real news sometimes'*, they held of news media, therefore, returning Mr. Brask's in-concise answer of, '*yes––but, also no*' for public consumption, was unacceptable, they needed to know, know for fact if their contrivance was indeed what he or his son host claimed it was, or could do what he purported it could on a recent news clip, or was it a hoax, just another corporate gimmick designed to raise awareness for entirely different set of products ---namely; those body lotions concocted in labs its manu-facturers often touted removed wrinkles on cue to retaining youth. They didn't much fancy reporting a product advertised in strong positive terms to do one thing but never does, or achieves an alternative result, such occurring here would amount to an severe blow on psyches or minds of hapless viewers at home especially on prospective elderly patrons everywhere whom franchisers of Yuug Behuul's dome could bet

TRANSMOGRIFIER
AGE CHART

detested being taken for a ride, except they were given a heads up: it was not as is.

In any case, if there existed even an aorta of fidelity in claims made here today by its owners regarding its ability to somehow do any sort of suitable good fit enough to warrant repeat patronage, then, there might be some room for reporting it in good light—even if all it was doing right then was bear down at them inside Redwood mansion.

But all things considered, there were no recollections of public viewership ever showing forgiveness for pharmaceuticals when faced with incomplete efficacy of medicine or medical devices, or for media or journalist reporting it, —they were certain failure in this regard wasn't enough to earn them such were they to report what ultimately becomes a hoax.

"It's true isn't it---Mr. Brask, whatever your thing to our right is, is able to make someone young again, is it true Mr. Brask?" —a hush indicating an expectation for an affirmative answer descended all around.

For an answer, Mr. Brask gestured toward his three young companions standing by his right, then subsequently at Mr. Jones, Mr. Canes, Mr. Ege on his left,

"Gentlemen, these six men with me have a combined age of six hundred ninety-seven years, making each of them on average a hundred-eight years old, but take a look at them, they have been re-toddled. Isn't it awesome how each appear like your kid brothers? ---Could anyone have ever envisaged a re-toddling transformation ever occurring?"

There were giggles, it had been a while since last time anyone of them heard 're-toddling', used instead of 'young' in a sentence, some said they never have.

Questions, or what passed for questions, were put forward to him in angry statements of *talk straight man!* ---but which were actually excited demands at Mr. Brask to be more concise in whatever information he was releasing he hoped they'd publish—considering how vital a topic it naturally was, echoed all around.

"Mr. Brask, you do understand we're media establishments, —we must report facts, facts only to our consumers. Could you be a little more concise in what you're saying?"

"But I am, how else do I tell it, or anyone say it for it to be believable? —these men may look a little older than teenagers, they are really way out there in age, ordinarily, you'd refer to them as—say, grandpa's, but hey, we have put them through it—with tremendous successes, like I suggested, none of us remotely expected what outcomes were achieved! ---Here they are now not just looking young, but young in all actualities; their genes, DNA, muscles, skins, ---except of course their; thoughts, memories, their experiences, those remain permanently unaltered in their minds which is where they ought to be, wouldn't you agree?" Mr. Brask continued, "---what you see behind," said he gesturing over his right shoulder towards his back, "---is called 'transmorgrifier', it passes light, a certain kind of light I am keeping myself from patenting lest patent office attempt to sell to another---you know? —ain't nothing new no more—" They had. There had been countless incidents of theft of patents right where it was supposed to be most safe, rending inventor and engineers at risk of losing their products, Mr Brask continued, "—Like I was saying, once inside it, light passes through one's body or that of an elderly person, or anyone above seven reactivating certain worn out or redundant genes, or those inactivated from birth, then activates some other genes in that patient's body, or should I say, —unlocks particular genes in mostly elderly persons---elders or seniors being ones most affected therefore are ones most likely going to be in need of it, upon detection his listeners seemed misunderstand or at least, disbelieved him, he enjoined, I'm speaking here of a kind of light capable of giving rise to longevity. Here, take a look over here for a minute---"

"Let me explain further," said Mr Brask almost nervously pointing towards a chart he wanted them to focus their attention on, "---it is like an artist using certain digital work tool, software's or programs, stacks layer after layer of unfinished illustrations on top of each other to eventually form a final image from his progressive layering, each layer representing different looks manifesting on one's face as time passed or age took its toll on a person as years roll by ---every one of which 'point in time or stage of manifestation continually mapped itself then record-ed additionally by one's DNA then stored till one day he or she looks old with facial wrinkles. Once a person enters into it for restorals, it begins a reversion of a particular stored layer of a patients person's facial manifestation during a youthful condition at a certain age, or a given period in one's life, to cause genetic return to a youthful phenotype, it begins processing towards a reversal, continuing it until a complete reversal of a patient to a selected or preferred point in his youth is reached, he, or if its a female, she, ——involuntarily commences healing

back to a mirror image of himself or herself observed of him then all in a matter of weeks, in many cases days.

In a series of activities which included walking over to a table between Yuug Behuul's tall dome and an adjacent wall, Mr. Brask unfurled a number of posters containing charts he'd folded into a tube half a day ago at exactly 10 P.M. on Sunday evening, he placed them on a portion of a partitioning wall he or whomever was bestowed charge over it thought reasonable to dedicate to displaying materials only moments after some reporters commenced inspecting it's flight of three steps on which every of it's others features sat, —noting it was from its topmost flight one must then proceed into it.

Further away from it was an electronic signage showing looping videos of all six transmogrification subjects consorting with strangers not present as they queued up—waiting for turns to enter into what they believed was capable of relieving them of age. Later footages of Mr. Brask's looping videos showed their emergence seconds to a minute later from its insides looking far more refreshed than when they entered a minute ago visibly different.

"Ladies, gentlemen, everyone, over here on this wall are images of all six men showing photos taken before, photos snapped afterwards, here, we have photographs taken now of each person, most prominent of which is Mr. James Clunky—almost a decade over a century years old , that's he farthest away towards where I stood minutes ago, take a look at where he's at now—" Mr. Clunky where he stood looking not a day older than twenty two, beamed in what was no less a childlike delight while journalists from various media organizations looked on at him in amazement. Mr. Brask continued,

"—That screen over there shows moving pictures of them, ---videos of their process of recapturing youth once again. Wouldn't you agree---? ---if a photograph speaks one thousand words, videos must speak millions, ain't it? From his continued usage of colloquial lingo, it dawned on everyone their host was one of such country folks with high premiums on honesty, if not, then—integrity. This seemed to have magically caused them to pay more heed while he addressed them, "---on these six seven-feet high charts here---" said Mr. Brask gesturing towards six charts beside loosely hung photos of his six subjects he referenced in his remarks. He picked one up, flattened them out on a board beside where a work table on which they were pinned, stood, he then said, "---you will see each man's name on top of his chart with a series of circles in lines of one thousand each---running vertically, it also contains horizontal lines you see here with forty wider spread circles, I'm sure you can---,"

"Go on---Mr. Brask, we can see lines constituted by circles," a chorus of voices assured him, they could indeed see it for themselves, Mr. Brask continued,

"What you see here are results of tests developed to accurately ascertain each subject's actual ages without themselves first declaring it. If you look closely you will observe each tiny circle summing up to forty thousands are hollowed out, but take an even closer look, let's see if any oddity might grab your attention: circles number from one to a hundred—eight have been filled out, in some charts, circles filled out number only a hundred-seven, in others like Mr. Clunky's, it is a hundred plus eight, Mr. Jim's—is a hundred, then four more circles, in Mr. Carpenter's which is our fourth or fifth chart, what is contained in it is exactly one hundred plus one completely filled out circles. Tell us what it entails---does anyone know, can anyone tell me?"

"Could you please say—Mr. Brask, what does it mean in relation to why we are here?" Questions of sassy nature like this posed by a man right after introducing himself by name, were hurriedly proffered to Mr. Brask in various ways, but he decided against granting answers to any other.

"Very well, indeed—I shall tell you shortly." Mr. Brask once again gave his assurances, then paused alternatively feigning activities on his desk, or contents littering its top, after which he scribbled down some writing onto his journal's pages without disclosing what—if any relevance his text had to answers he was about providing shortly.

When he began speaking again, he spoke of how they all were aware it often reaches a point when one realizes he is nearer his end than he was from whence his life began, which is when he begins questioning himself what difference or changes his being on earth brought to anything, —he wondered to their hearing if during this later stages, requesting extra time to commence efforts correcting errors made during earlier times in one's life, or at least to make contributions to humanity amongst whom he or she was given privileges of spending their live's duration, or see if he give a parting gift to this world his maker placed him, mattered at all, or meant anything. People agreed to his fine remarks.

Some declared it was very philosophical, some called it 'some deep shit', which in California's contemporary lingo, also meant 'an event or matter of great substantiality', others said it was mind boggling. A few declared it, 'true word' A voice mused how he'd heard it only too often, it couldn't make any sense to him any longer,

"I'd like seven volunteers, don't tell me your age---now, just seven of you, to step forward. I'd like to answer Zidan's, —I believe it's what you said your name was—" Zidan nodded his head, it was, "—I'd like to answer Zidan's question regarding why there are many circles, what they signify by a small experiment, anybody? ---anybody."

At first, six men stepped forward, a seventh, Dean Sheckles—a FOX man was going to, but lost his wits, turned back to his former position. Another man, wanting, —in all probabilities, to show how he possessed even more wits, perhaps guts than Dean Sheckles, volunteered quickly. He stepped out to join, making it seven volunteers, he too was willing to give whatever Mr. Brask was going to try on them, a try.

"Good! Now, I have six men, oh, —there you are, a seventh one." Mr. Brask was all smiles, he hadn't seen Mr. Sheckles advance himself a seventh volunteer.

All seven volunteers stood silently waiting for what comes next, theirs were assignments from reputable media houses detailing them to cover proceedings—a reneging of which was certain to be in violation of their contract terms mandating they make themselves part of whatever experimentation was in progress: to make writing better reports, publications or telecasting attainable, it might even earn quicker promotions; for those with questionable records, or are under censure following previous work malpractices, or those whose careers were at an end due to budgets issues, —their means of livelihood might just be saved— -if only they took one extra step to make a difference, hence these seven volunteers rose to push their lucks.

"Now like I said, don't tell me your ages, we are about to conduct tests designed to reveal what your ages are by way of charts like these hung here," he said to them pointing towards where reels of paper containing many circles hung.

Silence descended lower stifling every sound, along with it was heightened anticipation. Interestingly enough, Mr. Brask's own responses stunned everyone into cautious enthusiasm, they liked it, but decided to adopt a wait and see approach since proceedings were interesting thus far, to them, if what their host was trying to do proved to be true or any good, a great deal of excitement all over was sure to follow.

"We're in business, —who's first?"

"Here, Mr. Brask, let me go first, — what gives?" CNN's reporter being a man forever prepared to attempt anything including delving into uncharted waters where defective protocols hitherto ruled while corporate bandits roam—an experimental transmogrification situation such as this could ultimately turn out to be, if only to find out any newsworthy information, acquire a first hand determination of it's authenticity, or lack thereof, to report to his station, then eke out a promotion or keep his job.

"Very well Mr.---" Mr Brask hadn't knowledge of his name, he let his potential inquiry as to what his designation was, hang, "---in a short while I will show you your actual age on a chart like these."

"I shall accede," a resigned burly Mr. Painter—reporter from CNN agreed signaling his permission to commence proceedings of age determination without express declaration.

On Mr. Brask's behest, —Painter, almost pantomiming in similar fashion an entertainer in some magic show does, stretched out his
right hand, an upward peeling of his blue sleeve of his golf polo shirt
revealed his bare arm, an act that was inconsequential to any experiment
at hand since baring his arms was not a required protocol.

Placing his open palm on what passed for a tablet device placed
on its backside with its screen facing upwards shooting effervescent
light about two feet high above its surface. Yuug Behuul assisted by his
father after delegating it as a chore last an hour or two—put it there last
night whist arranging stuff.

In one or two seconds or thereabouts, effervescent light completely engulfed Mr. Painters palm forming a hologram around it
rendering it obscure from every eye fixated on it.

After pulsating thrice, it proceeded to brighten four times over,
moments later, a bluish line appeared—moving up then moving back
down across its screen. Thrice it moved underneath Mr. Painter's
opened palm in each direction before Mr. Brask announced termination
of experiments.

Seconds later, spectators witnessed what was a printer—not a
decorative accent on a wall nearby beeped into function. It's operations
commenced included printing on one side of a long unreeling sheet of
paper: measuring an undetermined feet in length—but two in width.

Upon closer examination, parts of Mr. Painter's unreeling sheet
already visible was filled with circles similar to ones found on charts
previously discussed, his age information visibly marked in similar
methods as those other test subjects. With Hewlett Packard continuing
to churn out more paper—transferring more information onto its
surface, portions filled with darkened circles along horizontal forma-
tion, in corresponding arrangement with blank circles lining vertically,
unreeled further, —it lowered downwards till all there were remaining
of space before bottoming out was a couple of inches.

Before long, all seven volunteers were through with age verification. As expected by Mr. Brask where he stood with a reel he opted to

first examine before handing it over to its owner, circles were perfectly blacked out, which to him indicated results must therefore be in perfect correlation with that particular volunteer's age, hopefully without showing a single degree of variance. With this first outcome guaranteed Mr. Brask, he beckoned them over. Moments after each man received his test's printout, there were shrieks of amazement. Test results significantly showed information none could ever find incredulous—a thing they all hoped so they could report 'headlines news', —what it all meant or stood for dawned on them. Many went berserk with excitement, they sang choruses of bewilderment, of awe till their voices—a little prettier than they usually knew how, were hoarse, —for what else? --- Joy! Joy! ---without cease, to note, there was not one, but two inventions at hand, one capable of causing longevity, another good at telling ages.

On these printouts belonging to each tested individuals, corresponding number of circles matching their ages were darkened. In utter bewilderment, it suddenly made sense to everyone there: it meant Mr Brask had not misinformed them over his six test subjects actual ages, darkened circles must then be their real ages.

Without further ado, no more pressures of any sort, Mr. Painter from CNN agreed he was thirty-seven years old---a number equaling that of darkened circles on his chart. NBC's reporter—in his prompt unequivocal utterance attested likewise: darkened circles on his chart corresponded accurately with his forty-two years alive.

American Broadcasting Corporation's reporter confessed how he could not lie about his age anymore, because fifty-six years was how long he'd lived on earth, clearly corresponded with fifty six darkened holes or circles on his own chart.

Before three more volunteers concluded making similar declarations of uniformity of their ages with darkened circles on their reel of paper, it dawned on everyone present, —transmogrifier---whatever it was, was clearly elongating life, then identifying, not merely predicting, ---actual ages of each individual processed through it.

Awe stricken, Billionaire Duran Buckler stepped forward pleading he needed to be certain there was no wool pulling over people's eyes, promising if success were constant each time, he'd be willing to allow himself undergo transmogrification after which—if it were no mendacities about it's possession of great potentials to make a gentleman like himself young again, dying in exchange for life's other more important more prominent or more permanent subject matters than merely being rich wasn't going to be an unholy idea. When asked to explain further, he replied how he being a rich man by any measure fancied investing his wealth into a new technology such as it, ---whatever it was, to make certain—not just only he benefited, but everyone everywhere around planet earth who was aging or had already aged, ---perhaps, become richer while at it.

Mr. Brask acceded to a test for him too.

A short while after sensors on Yuug Behuul's tablet device sensed his palm, his results on his own reel of paper began descending. Down, down, unreeled white paper slowly but surely, circles could be seen printing on it. When it finally ceased operation, Duran Buckler eagerly awaited Mr. Brask to tear off what portion contained his results. Returning back with it to where he stood, Yuug Behuul's father proceeded to lay it flat ensuring where test circles appeared faced upwards so he along with My. Buckler could count zeros.

Of all forty thousand circles shown, eighty-five were darkened. Duran Buckler clapped his excitedly, indeed, eighty-five it was his actual years alive on earth,

"Amazing---ain't it!" exclaimed he, "—simply amazing, just think about it!" ---Mr. Buckler added.

Almost gloating, it was Mr. Brask's turn to speak,

"What do you mean by amazing? —could you explain?"

"There are eighty-five darkened holes or circles on my sheet, eighty-five I must confess, it is exactly how many years---old—I am," he explained,

"---but, many more holes appear that are not accounted for, or darkened, what do they stand for ---Mr. Brask?"

Grumbling's spread, it was a question requiring a immediate answer, but which Mr. Brask's prolonged silence afterwards indicated was one none possessed courage to ask, it was one of those questions one felt ridiculous, seemed like a newbie—-amateur reporter, or sounded like a novice posing.

Answers to this question should have been apparent to all, ---or least deductible from facts Mr. Brask has studiously explained all morning, asking it therefore—-whilst not a waste of time, was unreasonable.

"You guessed it Mr. Buckler, those are latent years it has made possible—-"

"You mean your volunteers standing before us —-I for one think are no more than twenty, are nonagenarians made young again by—-?" —-he cut himself short to point at Yuug Behuul's great dome looming in a corner of Brask mansion's east wing.

"No, then yes. No, none amongst my volunteers is below a hundred years old not—nineties, over a hundred, —yes, exactly---Mr. Duran Buckler, it is exactly what I mean these men I emerged with from upstairs are all older than you are--- yet younger, believe it or not, albeit accidents, suicide, murder, executions, terminal illness, now have tens of thousands of years represented by each and every circle—ahead of them to live---all thanks to what we have behind us."

"In other words blank circles or holes—call it whatever, numbering in their tens of thousands—if what you are saying is true, are years one is yet to live, we have therefore, ---what could be a fountain of youth."

"Yes Mr. Duran Buckler, all things considered, I can veritably tell you we have what humanity has forever dreamed of, now given to us in its fullness here in America by 'Most High': creator of all there is himself."

Looking pensive, a failed attempt to hide his excitement Mr. Buckler filled with new ideas forming themselves regarding what he'd just heard, drew deep breaths to suppress his joy, he wondered aloud,

"But how can? —If I correctly understand is what your question is," Mr. Morsan Brask, himself clearly overjoyed with prospects of growth garnered Redwood mansion by Yuggy's feat of dealing with aliens from higher worlds, began, "---if you know anything about human DNA well enough, then you'd agree with me it maps, or should I say, ---it records looks, conditions of one's body or face at every stage one had been, then stores it in it's memory. Now, with--", —said Mr. Brask gesturing once again over his right shoulders to where his son's mysterious dome's presence stood, "---several events occur when one enters into it for what is ultimately, 'a rebirth process'. It's technology or sciences enters into a subject's, or patient's preferred age—where it is stored in his or her gene's memory, I mean, —that exact point in his prime, retrieves it back into his or her being," —snapping his thumb against his index finger in a show of certainty, Mr. Brask continued, "---boom!, transmogrification, a process of genetic restoration to a youthful condition is commenced. Not long afterwards, he or she is reversed to an age in his or her prime where a mirror image of their looks gradually comes into manifestation. Such patient or volunteer also attains onto similar vitality existent during primal periods he or she selected era."

For long moments, choruses of, *"amazing!"* echoed all around, "amazing!"

2

Silver lining:
Old folks anew again.

Times have since become different in comparison to when one last time checked, with every single social anomaly 2020's decade—enduring to it's middle parts, humankind—perhaps it's other creatures too, braced to welcome new realities of life: prominent among which was longevity's ultimate arrival with promises of opportunities to fulfill those life's dreams elusive in a human's short lifespan; but at what expense, at what cost?

Unveiling ceremony of Yuug Behuul's transmogrifier arrived, he, clad forever, —in memories of every spectator that spied him during that day, day's memorable events, —as just now, —in his tall magician's hat, conducted his duties satisfactorily, volunteering attendees held fast to their findings following successful completion of age verification tests, after which everyone was speechless how he provided answers to every conceivable question they took turns asking.

At events end, hurried steps removed every journalist from Redwood mansion of Big Sur, each with their unique thoughts, plans or agendas of what actions to take or what approach to use while reporting how they viewed proceedings––should they remotely hope to see their reports enable their respective networks edge out rivals or competition in ratings, moreover, Yuug Behuul's dexterity at answering question calculated to throw both he or his father off balance, made painted a look of unprofessionalism about them.

Some planned to report how they witnessed wonders in coastal California to potential patrons of young Yuug Behuul's dome was or does, it was like nothing anyone could ever remember seeing before, each journalist or reporter, ––he or she: planned to try explaining what good fortune has come mankind's way in their tell all books later on.

To some of them, it was time to branch out into careers sure to spring into being––that are relative to transmogrification, do some real dealing, associated with such business. ---'*This shit*': a widely accepted terminology quite a few of them variously employed while describing their present occupation holding them down or they were holed up in––wasn't up to par anymore.

Their blah blah blah musings to themselves or anyone willing to listen goes on endlessly: ––how they'd be damned if they failed to seek out some elderly rich person––carefree enough with his funds to enable himself with information about transmogrification, or its whereabouts, in exchange for a percentage of whatever investment into an enterprise relative in function to transmogrification––they're striving towards owning, ––after such old fellows own procedure through it supposedly convinces them either a direct or an indirect investment in it was worth not only their time––but efforts as well. In further fantasies, these journalists hoping for a book deal from Random House, hoped to do much more to encourage such old moguls to attempt a total acquisition of it come what may, ––then, everyone, including they: fantasizing journalist—-or potential authors hoping to reap where they hadn't sown, —by becoming certain enterprise's co-owners—by virtue of whatever percentages was bequeathed them by interested moguls now aged in years, for what amounts to a life altering information, —thereafter, visit banks with smiles on each of their faces regularly to make deposits of checks, for, it was an absolute fact no one could ever dare allow themselves age if a solution was at hand.

For little Morsan Brask, prepared in his fantasizes to grapple with fame, maybe even become rich too---after all, it was theirs, right there in their home—with neither rivalry nor competition, a machine they could do with whatever they wished since only they owned any of its kind on earth.

A whole lot of folks in Yuug Behuul's family's sphere of influence were saved from impending demise—given their advanced years but for immediate steps he suggested his father had taken to introduce relatives to his transmogrifier's technologies or workings, in advance of making it available nationwide for many a transformations to commence, 'rejuvenate' ---his father calls it, ---back to youth, just like his father's seven human examples exhibited during what proved to be a lengthy press conference on Monday.

Of late--- affluent—once elderly Duran Buckler, —himself transformed back to his younger self in his friend's or partners son's transmorgrifier not more than a month, —according to his father, no longer looked like he was a ninety year old, everyone circumstances handed opportunity to lay eyes on him now thought him a twenty four year old---he wasn't, —a man about town: twenty four being about half his father's age, though he wasn't too sure.

But anyhow, he decided on what he thought was a better option of waiting, as it was only through delays he could see what direction events turn from there.

Lying on his back beside his bed rather than spend time tackling his school math homework his father instructed he complete by noon, Yuug Behuul was immersed in thoughts—how: *It was exciting really,*

human relics according to his father, were no longer looking their age, some said,—they couldn't be differentiated from younger fellows recently exiting their teenage years. It wasn't just all about looks, they felt young too, —were actually young again now all things considered. All over—,' he thought', '—people observed them jogging about, undergoing strenuous exercises in parks cheered on in most cases by onlookers, ---their extra vigor sometimes imply—though several of them lacked whatever certititude it required to accept these young again's sometimes spontaneously embarking into making certain to outpace youngsters working out exercise regimes alongside them to prove a point.'

Monday's press conference continued to lure many hopefuls to Redwood mansion for weeks afterwards, they too were, —like those volunteers, or a handful of seniors already given a once in a lifetime opportunity to undergo restorals in Yuug Behuul's dome en route to reanimating them back to youth. They were seen at various places walking with, ---some swore, a swagger so—offensive, it came across like it proclaimed—

"Oh-hey, look, we're back!"

A lot of people were happy for them, save for an all encompassing swagger, it was too offensive—though folks were happy for them.

In fact, it's frequent occurrence—which continued to mount to embarrassing levels, alarmed Americans, a street patrol officer from a nearby precinct—in one particular case, halted a young again for a pat down for a possible possession of narcotics, ---a none existent protocol in their time, he initially failed to comprehend whether taking offense over his being searched was appropriate, or if it would pay off better to be nice to police officer Watkins doing his job, ---after all, all he or all other swaggering rejuvenants like him ever did to warrant such encounters with law enforcement in such unfriendly manner, was recapture youth after turning up at Yuug Behuul's door in Big Sur for a sun splash in his transmorgrifier.

His father, Mr. Brask, ---good hearted fellow everyone knew him to be, executed his part well. He paid unscheduled unannounced visits to numerous elderly retirement centers around California, intimating them of how all hopes were not lost, how there was now an, invention---call it whatever, or like he more accurately put it across on several occasions to what were usually no more than small audiences he'd managed to get to pay him some attention, ---'*our creators gift to mankind*.' Unsure of what to do with such an uncertifiable information, or how to respond to him, inmates would agree to return his visit to find out what his claims were all about.

Arrival to queues waiting in line for a turn in Yuug Behuul's where it stood continuously belching out a mysterious low growl legend associated with it was always prompt increased each passing hour. Once inside it, they'd have to make three utterances, or a certain utterance thrice, then wait for showers of a wonderful kind of light---for which there were no descriptions, but hoped to coined one soon then made available, ---but only, ---he surmised, when human intellect finally realizes full grasp of its nature---to be able to chose what words to use.

Yuug Behuul's rampant thoughts on how circular lights descended from it's topmost part, down, down, permeating all around a patient till his or her person becomes obscured from view, then lower to their feet dispersing all around, continued unfettered in his mind.

Thrice light showers fanning out towards its inner circumference cascaded downwards from its topmost part; a first, then a second, then a third circular effervescent lights, each time increasing in intensity, then poof! it turns off, all done with, a particular person's procedure finishes. Moments later, an elderly entrant's facial parts begins transforming; wrinkles diminish, lines on their foreheads, grow shallow, deep age contours, fill out, old fellows begin growing young again, ---in about a month, ---were unrecognizable regardless of how hard anyone---including family tried to correctly identify them, ---save of course by means of DNA test only, all from a process lasting no longer than a minute.

Duran Buckler in some ways grew into bosom friendship with them, he was always ---all in a few short weeks he'd been young enough again to be a friend, in tow wherever they went.

Together as usual visiting an old peoples home somewhere in

California---where all parties involved entered into agreement promising to never make any disclosures of a scheme of sorts until it was appropriate.

It was visit whose reason dwelt solely on recruiting more elderly citizens thithering towards an endpoint where nothing could be lost regardless of outcome or even if death chanced upon them during restorals of their youth genes.

Many, although, it was more like every one of them still nursed dreams of being centers of attraction, ---hence it still occurred to them to want to be noticed. Some were once reigning entertainers, mostly prominent actors decades ago---fifties perhaps sixties decades---passage of time had since settled into obscurity, ---were virtually forgotten, but were still alive. How each missed being seen proximately close to those good old Cadillac El dorado's with tail fins big dons of Hollywood, or other wealthy folks scooted around in during their time, or better still, ---during their prime when such flamboyant show of wealth mattered: '---ah, nothing they wouldn't do to have those El dorado's back again,' Yuug Behuul once heard his father say.

Since becoming young again in droves, such choice belongings as expensive automobiles began to matter all over again. Countless number of them owned swanky automobiles of their era they secretly parked; one in an underground cellar where it's features constantly remained

brand new, but was suddenly cruising around in it, another, was spotted speeding past everyone in an heirloom of an automobile three generations older than he was without a concern whether it rendered everyone in their position disagreeably out of place contemporarily speaking.

It was all there were to connect them back to their own time, after all, where were those good things of life promised them, now? —, like; Cadillac El dorado's, Lincoln's, Ford's, large mansions in Sunset Boulevard, Beverly or Hollywood Hills every one of them forever dreamed to someday be part of at some point in their life from childhood.

Others unfortunate enough to lack expensive keepsakes stashed away in private cellars, made do with retrieving bundles of their old clothing worn way-back-when—-they could no longer remember ever wearing, from; attics, basements, bunkers, or chests to put them on once more without daring to wash off any stale musk smells on it, ---it was oftentimes, a required necessity for fond bittersweet memories of good times past to come flooding back again.

Those whose only connection to their younger days was through exhume old neglected apparels abandoned years ago, some decades, hoping their old clothes begins assuaging nostalgia, were innumerable. Indeed, back on their backs anew, older fashionable apparels of past eras, not only transported them back to their youth, it gave them hopes to peer far ahead into times to come with readiness in their hearts, whilst simultaneously becoming telltale signs used by observers in distinguishing them from today's generation.

Nevertheless, it was only for now, their circumstances soon began changing given each young again's willingness to embrace ever changing trends in clothes they donned on to intensify their hunger to be snug in a second youth—more of which no one could ever halt now there was an increasing acceptance of Yuug Behuul's invention.

In various nursing homes, a lot of prospects too far gone in accepting fate, rested awaiting their time to pass without a word about Yuug Behuul's dome reaching their ears. Awareness, in what ever way it eventually occurred to any of them failed to alleviate any difficulties some senile ones with diagnosis of partial or complete loss of all facets of their cognitive abilities to grasp meanings of utterances reaching their ears, were suffering.

Comprehension of information about advancements in science foreboding possibilities of a second youth was beyond them, thus remained at loss, while those wealthy ones with clever children —it was discovered steadfastly withheld information about a youth giving machine's advent, hoping their wealthy relatives: some worthful of multiple millions of dollars, some of billions, a few---trillions, but were now confinement in nursing homes stricken with decrepitude, or had little time to live, —leaving vast fortunes these elderly centurions raised in their youths—a long time ago, establishing a constant stream of income to keep it permanent, amassed large volumes of it, then stashed it away, becomes theirs, besides, in what more or less summed into an extortionist's position of: —*who were they to live to own their own fortune? —it should be ours, or mine,'* —to coveting offspring or relatives, assets set to be inherited possessed more value, commanded more interest than it's amasser's life.

Morsan Brask confided in Yuug Behuul over their best buddy Duran Buckler's situation, —how he was fully reversed to his youth, was unrecognizable, therefore deserved privileges of being part of any renaissance business established to help many more seniors out of old age. Mr. Brask told Yuug Behuul Duran Buckler hoped to be given a chance to lend a hand.

Countless senior citizens continued to disbelieve even after Mr. Brask, his boy—Yuug Behuul---with Mr. Buckler sometimes accompanying them, visited nursing homes with factual information. When a few of them volunteered to give it a try during a previous visit, junior Mr. Brask quickly enlisted all five, then carted each away to Big Sur in private cars provided by their sons.

For two weeks hence departing their elderly people's homes for restorative procedures, their places remained vacant, fellows began raising eyebrows. When at last they finally showed in a visit—for each one's family put up a fight moments after re-emerging following termination of procedure, to reclaim them—preventing them from returning to colonies of aged people, they were virtually unrecognizable.

Severely embarrassed, a few were forced to resort to an even more unenviable conduct of swearing some loud oaths—up, some, down to their still aged peers to prove it was they removed a fortnight ago for processing. Two embarked into recounting secret wishes, stories, gossips they told each ensuring nurses walking about were oblivious of what was being talked about: for instance: how one moved most lusciously, or how it was only they she deserved, —how she might have been one heck of a lady after their own hearts way back in their youths, or, some other times, they bragged in their whispers how a particular girl, —a nurse there, was not their type.

None could be blamed for this outcome, following transmogrification, their peers appeared so drastically altered, it was difficult to recognize them. In any case, it began to resemble a distinct possibility to doubting Thomas's amongst inmates, —-they too swore they'd be damned not to seize any given opportunity.

From Yuug Behuul's understanding of what his father explained a few days ago, loads of eligible seniors far gone into dementia wouldn't understand what was amiss, —-except some quick actions like non-consensual transmogrification, were taken, their opportunity to recapture youth could slip by. Their children hoping on inheritance---ever ready to assemble a mob after anyone disposed to informing their elderly relatives about potentials of another youth, or even set caution aside to order a hit on such informants, were themselves often aware of similar plots by total strangers coveting wealth or resources of other families, harbored similar terrible designs on them, once their wealthy parent's undoing was accomplished; —there was, after all, fortune to be made by anyone capable of muscling everyone else aside en route to usurping fortunes amassed by another. Possessing knowledge of such wealthy folks offspring's reluctance to apprise senile parents of a

potentially life altering information, amounted to them, considerable errors in judgment since such error was capable of estranging them from inheriting fortune, leaving them permanently disappointed, was all required to goad them on, —relenting from a continual secret attempts by these covetous fellows at lives of senile mogul's greedy children, would be thought each frowned upon, —preemption to ambitious thieves where ever they were was sometimes all it required to come into wealth not due one, and if doing so to bad children—should opportunity---even for one fleeting moment, offer itself, then so be it.

News about some magical effects a strange futuristic appliance invented by some folks somewhere in California, or Wyoming—they were not certain which, brought into lives of many now called 'first volunteers', grew rife: it centered mainly on how a lot of seniors across nursing homes all over America—especially those mentioned just now, suddenly took on a different appearance. Prominent amongst which was how recognition of some treated peers—government agents, families or some other authorities took from various nursing centers to send over for renaissance proved impossible for many left behind, ---but it couldn't really be said for certain whether these rumors held water or not, —thus, —meanwhile, everyone cautioned themselves to be wary what information was accepted wholeheartedly.

Suggestions by quidnuncs they understood certain parts of rumors—where folks or seniors left behind at some elderly people's home only a while back could no longer recognize their peers visiting to say hello after transformation back to youth, was understandable, —since referring to any restorals' recipient as seniors—which they were when they departed, lacked veracity, —considering they looked like grand children in their twenties when they returned to visit.

Apart from tattletales were media houses—known to place blame entirely on government's constant tactfulness in carrying out one of those of its top-secret experiments with hallucigenics or psychotropics medicines designed to help seniors with infirmity cope with life in its concluding stages on earth—so that they could no longer remember recently discharged peers.

Young Mr. Brask, ---where he sat beside Duran Buckler---busy for a little over half an hour talking into his smart phone in such manner he evidently wanted everybody to hear his readiness to begin filming voiced out aloud, calmly observing proceedings. He was veritably grounded in with Mr. Mr. Brask, or his son, Yuug Behuul, ---an inseparable part of it all: an investor dating back to a couple of weeks, a co-producer: his chore among other duties, entailed making certain every sequential events of elderly folks arriving, or departing---visibly altered, were all filmed on video to be kept as record for posterity.

Through with figuring out how sales pitches could be made to TV networks, he planned to rely on his still vast reserves of cash to finance his involvement. To further enable his partnership, he secured a purpose built ultramodern TV production team in an ultra modern mobile studio to cover events, reassuring himself of eventual profitability of all his efforts he hoped was apparent to his business associates.

Bustle of activities by hired camera operators signifying Duran Buckler's entrepreneurial efforts were more apparent today when none including he, could manage anyhow to suppress mounting excitement all felt awaiting a new batch of volunteers from one old peoples home enlisted a week previously to be conveyed to Redwood in America's pacific shores along northern California coastline, it proved to overburden their minds.

Expected shortly, were former celebrities long past their primes due to advanced years hence have been rendered unfit for any sort of role in their preferred genre, or were now generally irrelevant, movie industry is now unable to find any more use for them, ---to, ---like everyone else, be given a chance at experiencing Wyoming's, or Big Sur's fountain of youth, a chance to find out for themselves if hoo-hahs surrounding it's emergence contained any truths in it, but more importantly, to recapture their own youths if it were true.

With these latest batch of former celebrities now willing volunteers, was one Mr. Jim Gainer, ---a fellow well versed in con artistry,

---at least in characters portrayed by him, was to a maverick extent, represented by his daughter known to possess no less of similar dexterity in her dealings in contemporary era, —a celebrity in her own right---with some usefulness still, it was said, embarked into furious lobbying ---even to high heavens for her dear father to be made young again, ---perhaps, even for a day, although, everyone knew of her scheme afterwards to lobby on for him to remain permanently youthful, not just for a little while longer should everything turn out fine.

Another fellow everyone remembered as ramrod of a famous cattle drive right after America's civil war in which those 'out of work soldiers' drove cattle through Indian reservations often incurring great ires. Though, not a member of Mark Rubman elderly home—a heck of a facility in question here, fortune was his to splurge on—it favored him in his youth, enabling him make good for himself, but he now resided here with them, he too like seniors all over, could not suppress his eagerness for a chance at another youth.

Another celebrity determined to defy nature was another female everyone knew, or were once acquainted with in one way or another in her hippie days when everyone took her to be a sweetheart, their doll, —too, wanted a taste of youth once more, promising to everyone's hearing—if Yuggy's dome—as some designated it, could make reversals happen—reverting her back to youth—when she summons up enough courage to accept going through with it, —early thirties being her preference, she'd go on to make better music, tweak banjos loud, sing country music way— better than anyone ever heard, —be it her own little contribution to making life easier for every folk she once denied, then reach out to touch them all.

Folks cheered her on like never before, resolving in their hearts if it were indeed true, she could expect their reminder of her pledges to reach back to touch them—for what it stood for, or how she must make good on them, —else, abandonment by all her fans till they were but a few left, was to be expected, her entertainment halls, scanty, then she, idol no more, but still---

"Way to go girl---" echoed people in one voice, to all intents her fandom was constituted primarily by men folk yet to find any contentment from merely listening to her music.

Senior Morsan Brask held on tightly, simply refused to relent or let his grip weaken till it was all over he was in full control of events. Be that as it may, it was little smarty-pants himself: Yuug Behuul everyone noticed whichever way they looked. He ran errands for anyone requesting one, but for a tip or token. He fetched bottles of water from refrigerators nearby---there were about six in near proximity, he repositioned chairs for twenty elderly folks in attendance to sit on, brought cups, tissues, napkins, et cetera, to whomever required it after shedding tears of joy.

Later, Yuggy took stock of how much running around doing various odd jobs or undertaking tiresome errands he undertook for visitors for others earned him, it was a little over two hundreds dollars given him as tips, —it was merely representative of a clever tact he employed to hang around for a first hand experience of old folks once again setting out to becoming young again.

Before an hour turned around, fourteen, —including everyone's doll, —though was a little distinguished regarding age. Of all twenty odd seniors present, ---each adjudged to have, —for their utmost advancement in years, arrived darksome boundaries where demise must take over from life, she was an only person yet to clock ninety, thus were more suited for an urgently treatment than she did.

Processing commenced, one by one they went in, after which each was informed about his, her being good to 'go', ---a word which in recent memory almost uncannily foreboded a promise for an untimely demise. To folks in their age grade, also a well known fact to many, 'going', to anyone beyond octogenarian years, represented 'dying'. — How they detested hearing it uttered in remarks with every bit of sinews in them.

"But Sir, —everyone's doll," —a jealous senior displeased over a much younger woman positioned in front of them, protested at once pointing out she hadn't quite entered where her end was nigh no matter what,

"Hadn't you said elders go in first? —what's up with her anyhow? —and, what's up with this 'go' of a thing, hadn't you said we were going to be young again, we don't gotta go soon, —do we?"

A quirky laughter-inspiring comments it was, old Mr. Peels was already talking slick much like he used to eight decades ago when he was twenty—even before it reached his turn for transmogrification.

"It's just an expression my dear sir, just an expression," Mr. Brask dutifully appointing himself coordinator to ensure a smooth processing of every senior, informed him.

"What about her, she ain't really old," protested Peels,

"She'll be alright," —Yuug Behuul in addition to his father's stated from where he stood, hoping dolly heard him. Thankfully, Mr. Brask's assurances effectively ended any disquiet threatening to arise over his awarding her privileges of going through her procedure before it was due her turn.

A bit frazzled from an active day of running around fetching all what not—all day, Morsan Brask; Yuggie, Yuug Behuul, struggled up from where he sat recovering from aches working hard put on his body to quickly intervene with a clarification of what his father couldn't find better words to explain, ---since their budding spring chicken corporation could collapse like a heap of badly stacked cards, or end prematurely in disaster for their side should their machine fail to deliver goodies their promises constantly led, or conversely misled every one of these senior citizens to believing was feasible.

"Oh, no, no, it's not what he's trying to say, what he hoped to convey across to you in his message is your eventual readiness to tackle life anew, —you know? —you guys are all set to go---"

There, he said it again, 'go'. Some seniors within ear shot hearing go repeated: a word to people in their peerage were unkind words, cleared their throats noisily: their own little way of registering their displeasure, Yuug Behuul quickly realized he needed to offer an explanation at once if only to ease their fears.

"What I mean is, he's saying you're all set, you all are going to be young again," he explained, "---he said, you're all on your individual paths back to youthfulness again"

There it was in that smarty pants statement again: 'going',—or be it said another way, '—*individual paths back to ...*' —only this time, disguised with finer words but still conveying what was feared most. ' *they just can't hide truths about it, can they?* Thought one aloud, ---but anyway, they understood Yuug Behuul's, hoping it was indeed it was what he really meant.

Reassured by it, everyone doll quickly cleared her process in well under thirty seconds feeling relieved. Soon afterwards, hers, in conjunction with in every one else's transformation began to grow apparent to their own naked eyes.

An old fellow, retired to a corner where he sat himself down to assumed, perhaps feigned an indifferent demeanor to others struggling for their turn, soon after undergoing his, though, he busied himself consuming spoonfuls from two bowls, one of custard—a close observer there determined suited his palate better than mashed foods of an unidentified nature contained in his other bowl, non solid foods they were—his circumstances of ill health, perhaps of advanced years mandated him for decades to adopt as a constant staple of his diet. He suddenly raised his voice in his declaration of how time was due he began demanding solid foods, he questioned aloud whether theirs: his family's or his caretaker's, —was a scheme to starve him to death, stating clearly he suddenly felt strong, healed, budding to move around as well without support. Following his outbursts, a deep hush descended, onlookers witnessed him muttering to himself. His' suddenly devolved into a nagging feeling he could use his legs again, a conclusion his blabbering couldn't wait to give away.

Of course, their witness of countless similar outbursts in recent weeks they'd been over exerting themselves lending youth back to seniors deserving of it, was quickly mounting in their memories, it nonetheless brought them joyous tears each time a senior surprised them with a reoccurrence. When senior Mr. Brask, then Yuug Behuul—followed closely by Duran Buckler whom none, except Yuug Behuul's father, could ever suspect was blabbering Mr. Mann's peer, himself, only just recently rejuvenated, urged him—through Yuug Behuul, to give it a try,

"Sir—," —began Yuugy, "—we'd like for you to demonstrate your walking skills again."

At first elderly Mr. Mann was going to ignore him, but thought better of it. Gingerly rising from his wheel chair he commenced attempts to exhibit his newly reacquired prowess at walking.

At first, it was a struggle to place his entire body's weight on his two legs caused them to wobbled, it was a feat alien to his capabilities. For twenty years—subsequent to a fall, he'd been confined to his wheel chair never being able to use his two legs, though—soon, he was standing upright, steadily taking what was no less a baby step after baby step. Back, forth, to, fro he marched numerous times till even he reached a conviction a priming of his physique by Yuug Behuul's machine, had either begun, or was complete, —what a joy for him to know he felt ready to tackle any new worthwhile endeavors—chief amongst which— he surmised, was adequately making use of his feet again.

Before long, another hitherto reluctant senior sadly recognizing time was nigh for him, convinced himself in an audible quibble, it was then or never, —how he needed to take chances at once, or he'd never again be able to: For upwards of three decades—till moments ago when two restoration attendants raised him to his feet, half dragging him over for his procedure to begin, sitting on his wheelchair was all there had been for him—by way of providing himself locomotion. But on this day, he agreed to be lifted onto his lame feet to drag him over to Yuug Behuul awaiting their approach so he could push his dome's doors aside for their entrance into it, —whereupon they tethered him to his wheelchair's upright backside to keep him erect for whatever duration he was required to say inside for his procedure to terminate. Both restoration attendants: men in their thirties, then raced outside, abandoning him howling—louder than he ever had—over his imminent fate—lest they— in their twenties, be reversed to their infancy, —their self centered argument being: since it could—fearsome—as it was, make a ninety year old, twenty, it could very well make them two.

Upon much encouragement from Mr. Brask, both men returned a minute or two later—at procedure's end, to find him still howling where he stood—though not as much as he had initially. They proceeded

to untie him amidst sorrowful apologies of having no intentions whatsoever to abandon him that way, before lowering him back into his chair
for onward wheeling outside.

Once outside, to everyone's utter surprise, they heard him—in
yet some more of those stunning tear jerking testimonies heralding
hope, dare them to unstrap him from his wheelchair's seat, —telling
them he felt he could walk. Without further ado, 'Senior', —as one man
refereed to him minutes before he was ushered in, determined to prove
himself, shot into an upright position,

"Oh, no!" —exclaimed he outwardly, "—doctors might have
been lying to me all along,"

"What do you mean?" —inquired Yuggy quickly coming to his
side to join in jubilating spontaneously in which some cheered wildly,
while thought it a ripe event for tear.

"Look, I can stand, I can stand, my legs, they're good," replied
Senior. It just wouldn't occur to this ecstatic Mr. Senior none other than
himself was all there had lived inside his body all these years, thus ruling
out every possibilities of any physician being able to lie to him his legs
were no good.

"Indeed sir, its been you living inside your body all along while,
have you forgotten? —no doctor could ever lie your legs are no good
anymore," a bystander echoed thoughts senior should have since allowed ruminate in his own mind.

Without any further hesitation, a thrilled Senior unsure whether
it was his fault forgetting how to walk, or if his crippling was conse-
quent upon his advanced years, took a tentative step, then another, then
another, then he like his other peer, really began to go about Mr. Brask's
dome room; sometimes in hurried steps, at other times slower; —here,
there, over there, down this way, up-stairs, down he came again, all on
his own two legs till he was convinced his to becoming a young person,
no more than one in his twenties, was well under way. He later confided
in close associates about a decade later his sashaying all over Redwood
mansion's great room, was his only way of proving to himself he hadn't

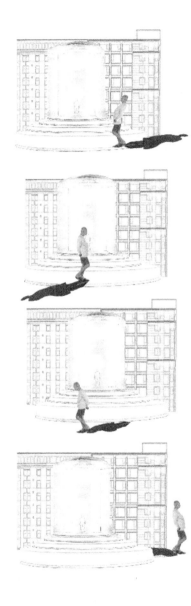

been inside one of those dreams wakefulness terminates, jolting one
back to a sad reality, he sometimes finds himself in memory lane
wondering nostalgically if it were still at that good ol' Redwood
mansion till present.

Closing time soon arrived, with it—-departure was contingent
upon them all to head for their respective homes, but another was to
suddenly halt everyone's round off activities when he shrieked loudly
upon gazing into a mirror he'd beseeched Yuug Behuul to fetch him,
—how a reflection he saw in there gazing back at him, couldn't possibly
be he, —then he commenced weeping—-thereafter queried everyone if
they were certain it was still himself—-while their comforting or reassuring of his overjoyed person—he was rejuvenating back to youth—-con-
tinued, one or two people witnessed wrinkles on his forearm noticeably
faded to its barest minimum, leaving him standing there swearing loudly
his eyes could see it fading,

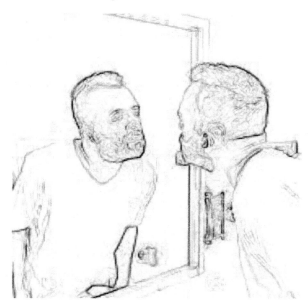

"Oh, my---!" —exclaimed he, "I feel different, look, my wrinkles are gone, look! ---there's one, its shrinking, its shrinking! It's getting better each passing moment! I see it! ---I see it! ---look, look!"

Similarly did another fellow, then a fourth. Before long, there ensued a frenzied kind of merry making that endures in Yuug Behuul's longings for a reoccurrence—even if it be in any other aspect of his life whatsoever, till this day.

There was a jumble of voices, some hoarse, some hushed by tiredness, others, age, ---all attempting to speak simultaneously but only managing shrill croaks, whispers almost too inaudible to hear, but in a short while since their procedure, were now once again sharpening in clarity, compelling a few to begin sounding off, evidently to assert presence, thankfully—though, it was all for a good reasons.

Too breathless to shout for joy seeing his constantly diminishing wrinkles every effort he'd made to remove from his face for over two, in some other cases—three decades, but met with failure, now suddenly gone, he along with all others experiencing similar spontaneous alterations, danced.

Ladies there led by Dolly, swore how after sixty years, —since their thirties, such resident anomalies on their bodies, skins, faces had finally met vanquishment, a handful of them, especially three furthest away from their end than everyone else---which naturally included Dolly, frantically waved their hands, or whatever they held in their hands, close to their faces to help evaporate some steamy sweat or whelming tears of joy threatening to fall from their eyes.

She being utterly delighted at eventualities, couldn't repress a sudden urge to make an ecstatic remark—later accounted for in countless testimonies of her uttering them; an utterance which ultimately capped that day's activities, when she announced to everyone's hearing,

"Hey, I'm back!" —it made everyone cry for joy, —or cheer wildly

During

Provenance of

Civilization

3

Excited creation:
A world below to discover.

*A*ntiquities ago, when earth was young, our world, painted a picture no better of nature's own atrium populated by strange dissimilar creatures mankind's creator 'Most High' placed in there. For their docility, it stood— stark of activities—totally devoid of eventuation's of any kind. Then gradually, there sprung into existence, first signs of activism lasting for all time.

First, strange sophisticated creatures busied themselves cavorting around it's vast reaches in wild excitement, mostly heedless of unexplained secrets preceding their arrival, then, considering great distances between its north, its south, its west from its east in which these creatures cast down to inhabit it must adapt their skills to nurturing it, it became imperative they pay attention to passing time, their kind's diminishing youthfulness on earth.

DON. M. DENN

To gain supremacy, creatures given strength asserted themselves too vigorously in what was their ploy to grasp hold of authority they must maintain even when absence of real threat or competition rendered it unwarranted, but, all very quickly, —calm ends too soon only for what must be done repeatedly to reoccur. He saw Divine ones continuing to behold spectacles it discontented them to witness: a refusal by some of creatures to tolerate any action any other within their reach in their box conducted regardless of its inoffensiveness, it was important to them to keep at odds with whichever deeds any of those other creatures set themselves about. Consequently, a fundamental difference demarcating good from evil, right from wrong, straightforwardness from it's absence, established itself as a main norm. It then devolved into far worse values for all in it, where, —for their impatience then, they could now only inherit for a short while before agedness tolled upon them, shriveling them onto death—only for life cycle to begin all over again.

Aloft this cardboard box, exactly at it's middle way on high, hung a lone electric orb before any of its inhabitants were created, born, then stationed at different points inside it, radiating heat downwards from it's vantage position to soothe their world.

Standing far higher, tall beings gazed upon all creatures, their visages forlorn, their appearance: color of ivory, their might many. Above them all stood one perceived at moments glance, to be; — Highest in rank, —Most powerful by stature, his hue: purest of quartz, or better nature that one knows not how it may be described. While each stood there in a dark surround universe, gazing down, many an idea it was that poured in from everyone of them,

"What doth we do with these—creatures?" —demanded each simultaneously, one paraphrasing another, still speaking as one in identical remarks, "these creatures, what may'est we fait avec ca?"

"We shalt—," remarked one being where he stood filled with readiness to apprise his standing amongst his peers onto greater appreciation by making his own opinion known, —even if a little,

"What say'est thee---" commanded him who is most in all things amongst them—to him who spake, —that all quaked of his presence where he stood towering over all,

"Do away with them all, but I shall say, let them be," —said he that spake,

"That which I have made? ---do away with them?" —even as he spoke, universes trembled at his voice's might, grounds shook, other beings bowed low, as for all creatures boxed inside their new world, many fled in terror, others to hillsides, one commenced a hole on earth's in which he shall hide, yet, nowhere they sought shelter, but vast open lands—welcomed them.

Yuug Behuul saw that thereafter, murmurs of discontent—as to letting creatures be or doing away with them all, spread on one side, he saw that opposing them were beings on a second side in which were whispers of approval or of agreement to doing away with all, or letting them be. He heard a great many beings laud both rhetorics as finer points than ever spoken by any other until one rose to speak saying,

"I shall see no need to destroy what Most High hath hewnt with eons worth of efforts, I shall beseech he for mercies."

"I shall accede. I shalt not terminate creatures which I have hewnt---" said Most High where he stood gazing down on all creation--that all quaked again,

"But Sire---," beseeched many divines, —except ones not filled with trepidation over what possible fall outs could manifest from stranger creatures dwelling amongst mankind in false semblances of man, complainingly,

"Silence!" Commanded Most High, "—Silence I say, for I shall call man thus,"

"But Most High, these be not man like our effigies doth be,"

"I shalt not tell thee again! —for I hath hewnt thee as I hath hewnt them—-"

"I hath sais, it is as thou hath commandeth that I fait ca, for thou hath made me scribe." A moment of what seemed to Yuug Behuul as time off taken to make verifications in some registry of sorts or oracle of this higher being's response to Most High, passed,

"I shall accede," said Most high when he spoke again, he had made it so.

"Aye, they are but effigies of man--- I hath sais, but, may'est we not deem them other designations? --- for they bear not our semblance, bear'est they?"

"Do not question thine creator—my servants, for I hath hewnt them—putting in them, souls – not akin to thine kind's."

"Yay---!"—howled creatures of closest resemblance to man appearance, gleefully, "Yay---!" —each of every one of them—showing happiness, joyfulness, gladness. They ran from within whence they had hid themselves in terror, into open fields to rejoice some more, where-upon to behold Most High's own orb placed high above to shower warmth upon their new world.

"But master, thou hath not finished---"

"Nay, I hath not,"

"Then, they are disobedient, they hath no patience," said anoth-er, "like he sayeth over there, wise it is we do away with them lest they grow wild. . ., Thou hath made me scribe as well"

"I hath sais I hath made thee scribe, mais, nay, for I hath hewnt them, I shall not destroy creatures which I hath hewnt, —for I hath not destroyed thee, yet thou et thine kind hath many misdemeanors—"

"I hath sais, pardon Most High, pardon,"

"I shall accede, mais, depart thee unto whence thine kind rests, lest mine wrath smite thee, mais, —I shall not."

Yuug Behuul saw this divine being lower down to realms below in his flight, grateful there existed an option to depart, —lest he be smote.

"But Sire—mine creator," said another, "—it perturbs many effigies this orb which thou hath placed above to shimmer light et warmth unto they,"

"Aye, for I hath not finished mine chore, yet these fled away from mine sight, —now, they suffer but little. It shall come to pass—I do away with all sufferings of their kind, mais only after I shall create another world whence only Aryans I shall send to dwell, et, these return onto another world. Still, he over there I shall call ape, that beast thither I shall call Bodach, he that is horned over there I shall call Boldakurus. he over there shall be Nigoh. Heckroyd—thou art I say. Regard he thither, I shall call he---Gonad, indeed Gonad another beast as Bodach be'eth, shall he be."

One by one each according to its likeness, each was bequeathed lasting designations to identify them for all time.

"But sire,"

"Aye, Gohabruh-Earl ---"

"These other creatures shall by their semblance, put into our creatures frights of many sorts, may'est we not put on them effigies of they thou hast hewnt? —for thus, our effigies shall not be a-feared at sight of hideous creatures."

"Aye, aye---" agreed sundry beings of on high,

"Thereafter, their maker shall terminate them still with geezer-hood, for they may'est not give their maker thanks for in them is a thankless dark in which they fled to hide themselves."

"Aye, Gohabruh-Earl, aye, I shall accede," agreed Most High,, "thee there, O'Barion Earl!," —he commanded,

"Sire, I shall accede—for you have called me." —said O'Barion Earl bowing low thrice.

"Mais, I hath not spake unto thee mine commandments—" Most High said to him,

"Still, I shall accede—whatever thou may'est say,"

"I shall therefore accede. Harken unto mine voice—O'Barion Earl—for I hath hewnt thee. Ye shall take every of their kind lying thither bathed in dust, you shall drape it one by one over all their kind, you shall put on them other hues of sorts---"

"But sire"

"Aye, Gohabruh-Earl,"

"For our effigies art few, let us make on to ourselves some fair unto our likeness to be companions to our effigies,"

"Gohabruh-Earl---"

"Sire,"

"Thou be'est certain thee shall not, being with them, harken unto thine own kind thoughts of thee, not of me, or of any other good I have done thee, thou be'est certain?"

"I hath not sais---,"

"Then, it shall not be wise we fait ca, I shall command each be placed according to their kind in worlds scattered all over many galaxies below where they may'est thrive in one likeness, no semblance of another kind shall perturb them, lest other kinds harbor in their hearts thoughts of evil, or of malice against thee, or against thine kind,"

"Then sire, we shall cleanse it out of them, their hearts shalt like Aryans hath it, be pure."

"Very well, let it be done."

"Master, I am O'Barion Earl, I have finished draping effigies of other hues, some hideous, some not, on many other creatures thou hewn'eth, now, non carry semblances---but of man, but although, Nigoh say'est, as Heckroyd say'est in loud voices---they hath multiple eyes, mais, they see'eth not more, plenty limbs they think'eth shalt make them stronger---before I hath draped them with effigies akin to man's, but they are yet feeble, thus, feeble creatures ask, hath thou authority to make of them into he who is handsome? ---but I pay'est not heed."

"O'Barion—Earl---"

"Master,"

"O'Barion--Earl, thou art servant, ---thou may'est prosper."

"Indeed master, indeed." —agreed O'Barion--Earl,

"Look, there's Bodach, there is Nigoh, no longer hath they curse of horns, tails, hooves---"

"---Master, for I have put on them effigies of our effigies they way thou commandeth, master---"

"O'Barion--Earl, thou art servant,"

"Indeed."

"There be Heckroyd, no longer does her anomalous nature show, but I hath eyes which see'eth what thou hideth—-for I am thine creator, but our effigies shalt no longer, et, I shall say to Gohabruh-Earl, thou art wise."

"Thank you sire,"

"But, their nature shalt be within they for they hath hooves, they hath horns, they hath tentacles, they hath tails still, they shall endlessly perturb thee Aryans as I have charged unto they to begrudge thee, until I shall resolve it."

4

Returning effigies arrive,
A second dismissal from on high.

*S*oon, but to effigies---hewnt merely of Most High's will, though, ---'soon' was centuries later, for days became weeks, weeks---months, months---years, years---decades, decades---centuries, till it was almost an eon, they returned back onto their little enclosure wise in many ways, wise in many things of their world---saying in mighty loud voices to ensure none missed his intended communication,

"Most high has returned onto his stead, we know not when he shall return," said a fearsome guard baring huge gates whereupon excited effigies drew nigh, with himself

"But we must speak to he, we must address he---for we are filled with thanks, to he we must give our praises for he maketh us good, in

his image we think," a fellow appointed their leader designated a name or title needless to be spoken of now, said.

"Go thee hence---" said he barring all haughtily, then he commenced simulating an action of prodding with rod of steel held ready to imperil any returned creatures should they not comply with his commandment to move further away.

It was a fearsome spectacle, for soon, a hand lowered from a distant firmament on high, with it was extended from thence to earth's terra firma below another rod of ion continually cautioning humans, compelling contriteness unto them, then a voice said,

"Thou may'est be proper, thou may'est be proper."

"Accordingly sayeth he---is it not?---we his creature he hath hewnt in his likeness?"

"I hath sais, still, thou art but creatures, he---thine creator, a creator of all there be---he is, thus, you shalt not have muster to return unto he when thou please'eth, ye shall harken unto his voice, do thee all he hath spake, lest all thine kind be smote, then, hewn another---he shall. Mais, I shall yet tell he of thine gratitude on to he---"

"Kind sire, we beseech thee shalt tell he also warmth from his orb which he placeth on high shall be reduced---for we burn, shall ye not? ---except it be lake of fire or of brimstone he hath hewnt for penance--- which he spake of, is it?"

"Burn thee? ---his orb which he commandeth to soothe thine world---burneth thee? Aye, burn you shall, for thou flee'th from his sight unto thence before his task of creating thee---all thine kind, all there is, hath ended, that thou may'est see for thineselves with thine yeux where else he hath created, for all thine kind to feel for thineselves also, ---Gohabruhi---Earl's earth onto which he may'est lower thee, ---even before he hath secured thee with armament of cloak which doth sheathe from furies of it, now, thou hath fetor at might, speak'est loud of woes, or of frightful maladies I hath not sais. Go thee hence I say! ---mais, I shall convey thine greetings onto him lest I too be found afoul of his ordinance or of his commandments---it shalt make me not worthy of his sight."

"Great one, thither where that creature rested over there, why hath he made them thus? ---umbra of hide, colored not in fashions of any good of nature?"

Howling mightily in laughter, he regarded them all with sad pity in his eyes, he said,

"What effigy thine eyes perceive of they now hath more good over semblances all their kind hath been hewnt of---before all thine kind fled unto earth---from whence thou hath returned. Thine kind shalt have perished from fright to behold their true natures which he doth cloak with that effigy of man, ---ah, thee---ants, thou art still without courage of my kind thine kind may'est s'appelle 'giants', mais, even unto our kind, their nature which they hath before, hath many horrors I shall a-fear till I shall be no more---thus, I shall remain contrite in my deeds lest Most High curse me like he doth they." ---then additionally, he said, "---thee hath more creatures in thine earth living inside effigies of man far more hideous---I may'est not speak of for I shudder to tell thee."

"We shall accede, thou hath spake well," mortals suggested to his hearing through their spokesperson well versed in mimicking native dialects of realms of giants.

"Alas! ---thou hath not remained till Most High doth terminate his chore to hewn thee, ye hath not received his gift to see countless centuries, era after era, with thine eyes. It shall remain so till he shall bless thee with many years thou may'est trouvé out of his transmogrifier, et, his regressifier, et, his perpechuafier---whence upon he shall give them unto thee. Mais, I shall tell him of thine gratitude---"

"Say unto he, we beseech thee---great one, ---thus say'est his creatures Aryan he hath hewnt by his will, ---we set off to discover earth---our new world; it's hills, it's valleys, it's plains, many of it's beautiful prairies which he hath promised us afore days---not more, before we set out, ---to marvel at its glories, its goodness, whereupon we visited great waters, streams, lakes, vast forests, regarded wondrous fruits on trees reaching heavens which he hath hewnt to give us succor when he shalt put us thither. We hath also set off to see other places, but we shall have returned upon him to be grateful, to give him thanks, to praises his name, but alas!, —we find he depart'eth sooner. Now, we know not what must do." beseeched Aryan leader, "—tell him kind one, we beseech thee, oh---please do."

"I shall, I shall tell he of thine exhortation, thine wishes, thine pleas unto he—which thou hath spake, for even I hath helped procured bits from which he piece'eth thine kind together, like he, I hath not wish for your destruction. Je pence thee be'eth well. Be fruitful, be thou patient to await his return upon which he shall bring forth more gifts through which he shall bless thee all bountifully---"

"We thank thee oh—great one---" said Aryan spokesperson wearied as he was, still joyous like all his returned brethren.

"I may'est now depart, I shall tell he all these things thou hath spake, what be'est it he sayeth, I shall bring unto to thee hither."

"Wait, before thou leave'est, kind man, tell us, art thou—?"

"I am of Gohabruh-Earl, son of Most High, mais, I am thine master, thine caretaker for any eras Most High shall make me such."

"We shall not doubt thee great servant of Gohabruh-Earl, but I gotta tell ya---." At this juncture, Aryan had either run out of diction of giants, or he had forgotten his line, thus was now speaking ill begotten grammar wont to creatures of his world.

"Thine ethos is---," —mortals could just manage to extrapolate meaning from muffled musings of a second great being not far off, but was till loud hence it carried across to their ears.

"Very well, thou may'est speak, I hath sais thou art Americoa," acknowledged great one,

"It ain't gonna be easy, but I can assure you, we are your wards---you say we are, —Most High's creatures, ---hey wait a minute, we hadn't set our eyes on him, he's sure going to be pissed, ain't it?"

"Ha-ha," laughed great one, "pity you young mortal, thou may'est not speak of thine creator with thine unholy ethos, lest he give thee bitter chore thou may'est fait before thou shall proceed," said he, "—et, thee shalt not lay eyes upon him thine maker of all things, except he shall accede, ---lest thee be made blind---"

"Very well," agreed Aryan spokesperson, "---I let glimpsing of him be, lest I be made blind," added he, "—tell he when thou depart to return unto he, "we shall not falter, we shall not lose faith in he, all he giv'eth unto our kind, we shall be grateful."

"It is well, keep thine faith in he, it shall be well."

With these parting words, an earthly world doomed unto mortality went on to retain secrets of its beginnings in conjunction with a continuation into dark uncertain future.

Still engrossed in his dreams, Yuug Behuul realized numerous questions posed by passing generations of excited earthlings lowered unto it to discover it's mysteries, far outnumbered all available answers by a ratio of infinite number of variables to one, —for earth remained a place of ancient secrets of creation, —a place where for a long time afterwards, or---at least during eras following their descent onto it, unavailability of answers—remained a great comfort to everyone, eventually lending peoples of Unisto Statazoa Americoa—-given charge over it—following their premiere placement thither—whereupon they established a civilization others must follow, —a place where for their contriteness, elders would one day find a second youth.

===   ===   ===

Ten-year-old Yuug Behuul awoke from his dream in which earth's secrets, perhaps, knowledge of ancient mysteries at onset of time were revealed to him, glad Duran Buckler, reverent billionaire—himself a beneficiary of his fountain of youth—allowed usage of his family name *'Morsan, Brask, even Yuug Behuul'* at appropriate times for business purposes or publicity, was still with his wealth, but more importantly, had now acquired an experience with restoration back to youth, both of which aspects were a good set of resources for subsequent eventualities regarding their pending business venture.

Racing off to his bath, promising himself he was onto no matter how much work was pending—requiring immediate attention if earth was to live on, recapture its youth, not shrivel up unto death.

Pledging to himself to make all those regrets of failed lives, or of human's own apologies to human kind for insufficiency of time to accomplish all one could ever desire in one's life he often heard his father, Mr. Brask talk about, a bygone issue. He knew it—he knew it—now, if only he could give it his best from now on.

5

Recapturing of youth,
A new kid in town

Transmogrification, or, —regressification: for there once again chanced upon earthlings another newerfangled sort of trasnmogrifier it's makers christened '*regressifier*', —which every intended senior now preferred for use in their own personal reinvention for its smooth operations often known to yield near instant results. For quite some time lately, procedures of recapturing youth for interested citizenry with it, proceeded everywhere they were conducted unfailingly.

Numerous units of this newer instrument of youth—which themselves were made superfluous in number by yet another new, or at least—a yet unknown process named '*replication*': by which means a replicator, —which incidentally, resulted from whence transmorgrifier or regressifier arose, —but whose discuss we shall allow become topic another time, is an approach to manufacturing entailing a unit of, or units of tangible of goods, —placed in a tall cupboard chest, after which all obscure scientific operations inherent within its system or technology commences functioning by way of ionic manipulation of atoms usurped from what tangible goods placed inside it for replication, it then proceeds to recreate an exact, or preset numbers of exact copies of any matter or item to be reproduced.

A great asset it could be for illustrious, industrious entrepreneurs, but for now is hoarded by its creators—they said shan't have it, —in their resolution in keeping it their secret till time shall pass.

Flawless distribution of these transmogrifiers or regressifiers, —themselves replicated into plenitude by a quick replicative process, to different districts across America—starting from day one till it was all over.

There were three in Idaho, six in Texas, four in New York, eleven in California, one or perhaps two in State of Washington, another two in Washington DC. Units were hurriedly rushed out all over, making little Yuug Behuul: Morsan Brask—along with his buddies to emerge house hold name everybody talked of ceaselessly. Everyone remained upbeat about it's continuous spread—promising to everyone's hearing, *there's more where that came from.*

Theirs was satisfaction over their good deed, ---following initial trepidations they suffered at first, to find what was afore thought—a daunting task of undertaking basic tasks of ensuring   distribution —which eventually turned out to be a successful accomplishment.

Operational robustness in allotting pods to centers across America followed Yuug Behuul's certitude in recruiting his best buddies; Toman Taner, Nathar Saller, Robart Foral, Mark Earldomeed, Jon Bradelwood, —not excluding Ando Campiron: a peer of theirs assigned dissemination of information to everyone within earshot—his grandparents were transmogrification procedure beneficiaries. In his doing so, he let people know their decision to proceed favored transmogrification—an older method, over regressification: a later but more efficient, or more rewarding process, because to them, a lot of their: associates who'd already passed through it were comfortably in their thirtieth year past a hundred, —but to anyone encountering them afterwards, they could not be beyond their mid twenties, for this, they repeatedly rationalized there were no better judgment or action more sensible than sticking with what was tried, tested, true. Ando let his listeners in on his grandparent's promises to try regressifier later when it too proved its worth or mattered more

None too pleased with his son's publicizing of family affair Danny Campiron, Ando's grandfather took every measure to curtail his son's ease of delivery of privy information to strangers, but there was a contract tem he must abide by. It was learned from their grandson's continuing anecdote, preferred calling it; *'a passage: their passage through a friend's fountain of youth'*, after which their rapid transformation into an exact semblances of their personalities in their mid thirties, though grandpa Campiron image or appearance still resembled a fifty year old: his procedure a couple of days ago in a nearby center was too soon for any outward magical transformation to reach completion, —for now, he was still rejuvenating, his family knew he was certainly going to be forty, maybe even thirties---soon, —it was left to be seen. In any case, both elderly Campiron's looked half their eldest septuagenarian children's age, one being Nick Campiron—Ando's father, in all, a very wondrous occurrence if considering grandpa Campiron was a hundred-six years old, while Ando's grandmother was a hundred-two.

Yuug Behuul's *'little quartet'* sufficed a title for Yuggie's father to designate his son's group of young enterprising lads, were there only four, but three more—comprising additionally of Toman Taner, Nathar Saller, Robart Foral all of whom were three more of his son's friend's.

It was during a photo shoot beside Yuggie's dome such a name suddenly flashed through his mind. But their numbers swelled to seven after three more friends ---urged on by their own fathers once it was apparent good prospects surrounded their appearing before TV cameras beside a tall round glass mechanism, to enlist.

Each father newly enlisting his son fancied how their son's friend commanded attention on a recent show—swearing up to high heavens then down back again to earth—was brought to him in his family home by what he sworn even more fervently were some other-worldly being bearing designations he wouldn't know how to pronounce---regardless of any efforts he made, ---though—several of those apprised of this funny anecdote of Yuug Behuul's, reminded themselves in their private quarters it was more likely some fear in little Yuug Behuul's heart over mentioning names of strange beings lest hearing it cause them to return, —not least—according to his further testimony, —when their appearance left him lacking comfortableness all day. His knowledge of their

eagerness to return in an instant was absolute, —it was, after all, their 'tall dome' reactivating genes, recapturing youth, then giving it back to elderly folks all over: people in their eighties, nineties, even centurions unexpectedly becoming youngsters again: —people seemingly in their fifties, or forties, even early thirties in some, ---but no less, ---though a report once erupted of one man, a fellow in his late nineties reverting to what was once his mid-twenties. People agreed with him upon seeing a photograph of he then: a little over seventy years ago easily mistakable to be a photo of him snapped not more than a week or two past, had it's lack of color not betrayed it's era, —'*who would have thought,*' was word about town.

Their number swelling to seven, compelled Yuug Behuul's group comprising he, plus his six cling-on's, riding a boss's coat tail,—his, to settled for a less fancier title: '*Young gang*', on his behest of course. At their young immature ages, bearing self-aggrandizing titles mattered very little whatsoever, it was therefore not a worrisome issue to young gang's members.

Young gang's chores became no more or less posing in front of cameras with their leaders great eight story tall dome, —units of which were increasingly being installed in centers across America, just behind

in every single occasions Yuug Behuul's 'Young gang' honored an invitation for a press conference with a visit they'd be intimated was designed to lend more substance to domes installed in a center operated by an inviting host, —which, it, —like every one of its kind everywhere else, were now generally revered as symbolizing; youth, vitality, hope, healing, even growth, with their presence by it during interviews.

In spite of their increasing fame, they were more often stationed in Big Sur California where it all began---until an invitation, any invitation from any media organization, or centers franchised to undertake procedures, arrived their desk. Off they usually went in search of fame, or to honor it, though, corporate endorsements were not to be missed, nor were sponsorship payments, —boy! ---were they having times of their lives! ---whilst relishing widespread attention it all brought their way too.

They held on fast to their spot in news cycles, remaining a hot topic where ever one went for month after month, although, a contract awarded a glass sculptor in New York city to construct a much smaller transmorgrifier, —whose appearance was very much similar to ones in restorals centers, but measuring just one foot wide, by three in height, —by Mr. Brask, —it must be said, eventually reached media houses reception room following a series of experiments conducted without publicity, ---or government's knowledge by its owners stunned out of their wits, once they realized leaks, —of what they held closely to their bosom, to news organizations from unknown sources to have really spread widely, nearly eclipsing young gang's celebrity standings or that of Brask operations entirely.

For networks, it soon became a matter of serious consideration often resulting in indecision regarding which story; 'Young gang's or 'stories about ageless Mayflies', viewers tuned into more, or could attract more commercials, be more lucrative to report to an insatiable public seeking more, or to gain more ratings.

Procurement of Mayflies, a species never known to last a moment beyond a one day's lifespan to process for further experiments, set trials to prove longevity was a possibility into motions. Not one day later did it terminate, not two, nor was it seven, or seventeen, nor a hundred–sixty three, but two hundred-twenty seven days later, yet, all forty-seven mayflies processed through two little transmogrifiers in a pent house in NYC Yuug Behuul family owned, continued to thrive, none had yet succumbed to any illnesses, nor perished.

6

Research fellows versus

a panel of inquiry.

Two hundred twenty-two days, concerned researchers figured to be human equivalent of twenty-five thousand years all forty seven test creatures lived, stunning societies of scientists confronted with such an incredible outcome. One day, a sultry twenty four hours following commencement of experiments was all they'd expected before termination. This astonishing nature of result caused quite some doubts in government quarters, officials questioned wether scientists paid top dollars to fetch these flies from their comfort zones for experimentation were not onto some gimmicks of they hoped weren't discovered.

In all their years armed with degrees enabling their pursuit of science careers in various disciplines of biology, of zoology, —chemistry, animal sciences departments, unsung assayers involved in these longevity experiments later testify collectively before panels of inquiry instituted by all three tier's of government's regarding reports of Mayflies never living beyond a day. When all their testifications returned accordingly, each was again assigned second chores: this time, to verify if tested creatures—still very much alive in custom nests constructed for them, were truly mayflies---not some other creature clever scientists—or lazy ones hoped to pass off as Mayflies in their want or need in misrepresenting facts—so as to keep career's going, or at least, to receive handsome wages easily without undertaking any arduous tasks of conducting any scientific research grueling whatsoever.

When all their responses again affirmed their knowledge those were certainly either mutant species of Mayflies capable of achieving longevity on their own volition, or, it was some unrecognized effects of unprecedented sciences within table top domes used for experiments causing tremendous extension of lives of all tested Mayflies to occur; it widened every bit of conundrum surrounding it.

In attempting to halt or remove a deepening mystery out of a confusing topic of life beyond what was genetically possible, all tiers of governments or their agencies involved invited their own scientists

theretofore assigned high prestigious titles: 'seasoned scientists, experts', ---howsoever they were seasoned beyond ones already questioned---it was not known nor were they willing to say either. Their procurement was for each tier of government's own purpose of an in depth investigation by collecting DNA from all forty-six remaining antiquated Mayflies—one having died from being accidentally stepped on when it fell right next to a scientists shoes, to reach trustworthy conclusions for themselves—whether these were indeed Mayflies or not.

In any event if even one winged creatures lacked necessary identifying features or characteristics of Mayflies, —they were prepared to begin preparations for stringent prosecution, charges of fraud, or attempted embezzlement of government funds: salaries paid scientists by way of salaries, or for deliberately providing faux manipulated results or reports for publication by government, then see where it takes everyone involved. Obtained results only served to deepen every facet of mystery surrounding it—it set out to resolve; verifications by scientific tests from numerous laboratories through their individual findings those were Mayflies were returned.

Disaster averted, all three tiers of government prompted further advancement of experiments to in-depth levels: a series of events—entailing reaching ascertainment whether any contracted scientist or their laboratories possessed knowledge of existence of any other species of Mayflies—or any other kind of flies for that matter—yet to be subjected to rigorous tests, they also requested a thorough research into whether there were any other dependable test procedures, ---even if they were of differing experimental approaches from what was currently in existence or acceptable, —or be it still in its infant stages of approval by appropriate governmental authorities, remotely applicable in reducing test findings to a final conclusion. This injunction by governments' effectively reverted matters back to scientists.

When all there was were nays, these intrusive governments already equipped with answers to their scientific inquisition once again tried their skills with another method of extracting hidden truths sometimes held privy to practitioners of certain professions whose perpetual mantra included sole knowledge of certain facts which they—-according to their union's manifesto, swore to never tell, ---a tact governments suspected involved scientists may yet have employed. It became apparent relations between governments' on one part, scientists on another, were not as cozy as thought at all.

On learning state government's for some reason presumed science establishments was out to hoodwink them with a deliberate---perhaps not, ---stream of constant misinformation, people relented a little to see what resulted from of it, crooked scientists could expect some unfriendly eventualities just ahead should they be found wanting in integrity.

'Impossible, how can? ---a creature never before known to last beyond a day suddenly lives hundreds?' These findings encouraged them to remain firm, hold fast on their position, subsequently assuming a hell bent attitude on recovering their money's worth regardless of efforts of governments'.

7

Revealing of a Young Grandmother.

*D*uty called, ---Yuug Behuul's young gang led by every kid's ever eager idol, ---though any, seldom admitted it in school cafeterias, ---celebrity extra-ordinaire, California's own Yuug Behuul or, for purposes of clarity, Morsan Brask, but he was still everyone's darling Yuug Behuul beloved by all, again went forth answer.

Many of these invitations were facilitated by ad hoc organizing committees appointed by media networks to ensure Yuug Behuul's 'young group' were home or at any place officials could reached them sooner for quick availability for interviews, a situation preferable to their being somewhere unattainable, or playing about---thereby inconveniencing media house staff searching for kids---wasting good talents snowboarding, biking---or generally soiling themselves in way their peers everywhere were often want to do.

They all knew it, they all knew frolicking around was 'young gang's' preferred way of spending free time—were all things equal, sadly, for these special kids, especially their leader—Yuug Behuul, it wasn't to be, precautionary measures of monitoring their minute by minute whereabouts became their fate since no day goes by without there being an urgent need for a paid photography session, or sponsorship offers requiring their presence—nobody partaking in young gang's lucrative publicity act they all voluntarily signed for, wanted to miss out on ---for, notwithstanding their efforts, cash, ---like in times gone by, was still hard to come by these days, —was still king.

During one of these occasions difficult interrogatories were posed to scientists returning their mayflies for verification, Mr. Brask, his son Yuug Behuul, then Toman Taner, among many others, were amongst what came to be known as 'well meaning citizens' invited to join TV interview session: they too were to lend credence to their past remarks, or provide answers to questions about current happenstances surrounding transmogrification, —their dome, then furnish viewers with opinions respecting what their young minds thought America's sudden on-going cravings for youth generally symbolized.

Once a particular session commenced, sparks would fly forth from interrogators towards their cornered guests; —Answers hitting them back from those providing them, lacked neither conciseness nor a failure to match every aorta of forcefulness with which questions were fired.

It, in Toman Taner's feeble mind, perhaps in his friend's—Yuug Behuul's, symbolized good tidings for young kids in their peerage, their families---maybe their immediate forebears---if they still considered themselves young, an entrance into a 'big dome' guaranteed everyone of them lasting youth accompanied by utter longevity, it would also ensure another youth for grandparents all over, —though, nothing like 'young group's every member's mean age---which if considered was nine, but you know? ---Toman Taner refrained from commenting any further, so did everyone in attendance—all of whom understood him very well, his explanation being clear enough.

For Yuug Behuul, 'young gang's most mature member, ---a maturity not attributable to his understanding of matters---for he hadn't much other children couldn't fathom, but because during his upbringing years—which still proceeded smoothly, his father, Mr. Brask made it a point of his own duty to constantly wheedle ableness to see things differently into him—as was this national issue presently under review, —alongside constantly doing his home work each day after school.

Explaining away his understanding of current affairs, it was revealed, he possessed knowledge it was good for what his father called business prospects, —for human being's own outlook going forward, how he understood a second chance at youth—transmogrifier's unearthing was heralding America's aging population to live much longer, perhaps long enough to take advantage of hitherto untapped opportunities to achieve reasonable outcomes in their lives—worth remembering. Of course, surmised everyone listening, his fluent gibberish was no less what his father taught him, though, it made sense.

In continuation, Yuug Behuul, still addressing press people while they busied themselves scribbling down whatever parts of his speech was apprehensible, —talked of;

"How old people, elders—" he quickly corrected himself before anyone took offense, "—now had a chance to last far longer than ever before because of transmogrification, how they'd just live on, have more strength to do all sorts of stuff till maybe; twenty, thirty thousand years, or possibly what his father called, 'beyond', before time arrives for anyone to —," he let his words hang.

On investor Brask's behest: processes of his', along with that of his senior corporate partner's relative's transmogrification, entered posterity through recorded videos containing footages optioned for viewing pleasures of all interested in seeing it, or reserved as necessary proof of their claim transmogrification inside a fountain of youth came about through them, should a need to prove it arise in later years.

These videos were supplied freely on each of these occasions of interviews or interrogatories, to friends, associates, lastly relatives of relevant persons unable to neglect previous engagements for a place on a show, to cater to their viewing needs or pleasure later telling them to,

"Let others know––," or, "––tell your grandpa, or grandma."

Of course, to everyone––according to stories, transmorgrifier's development, ––howsoever it occurred, was by young Yuggy perhaps his father––he, Duran Buckler couldn't care less, perhaps hadn't bothered to find out, was but a mere investor out to satisfy his guilty pleasures of seeking out fortune from whatever scheme of things there were about.

For his honest nature, Duran Buckler barred thoughts of usurping attention deserved only by his father-son colleagues from his mind, he could scarcely suppress his own anxious desire to be part of what he foresaw being an utterly lucrative venture––that prompted him to enter into a dicey arrangement in which he involuntarily agreed to use several Brask names alternatively––but when relevant, so there was no use spoiling things for himself with sinister plots.

It however was no less a gamble Mr. Brask devised to keep his family's integrity intact while still permitting he––Duran Buckler to confidently continue being part of it all, ---if assuming a new alias was all it required to make himself part of a blossoming new perspective of raising income, moreover, regardless of how much he felt obliged to his employer---using of their name as an alias, this engaging business of belonging to several novelties or goings-on; impending fame, potential fortunes to be made, on coming celebrity status, et cetera, suited his ego tremendously.

It was one of only few chances he was willing to take, after all, his own name: Duran Buckler, which could have become a household name in nineteen-fifty-eight, or nine, perhaps until later into nineteen sixties of last century, but finally did in twenty-eighteen when his lottery ticket was at last redeemed, was to his utmost chagrin, synonymous with gambling where ever they talked about him: though a gambling not consistent with pokers, but with fate, considering it was merely a childhood negligence a long time ago just outside of his infancy—like Morsan Brask, when he simply bought Idaho's lottery's winning ticket in nineteen-fifty-eight, —failed to look at it for decades, but later invested his winnings wisely upon discovery of his ticket inside '*Old faithful*' his pink piggy bank which he still owns till now—never letting it out of his sight again, —studiously saw to it his enterprise prospered. Retention of enough finances from his businesses empowered him to take advantage of an unavoidably tempting option to invest into a venture he foresaw to be a most lucrative of ventures set to give youth back to senior citizens. Like Yuug Behuul making certain promises over what he barely understood, hazarding, —he often reminded himself could never be far from any of his undertakings: a trait by which his associates knew him well even as a child; —it was more so now given how he plunged right into this joint venture without consulting experts learned on issues of aging. It was only after coming to fore—that he learned from gossip, gambling was one sole trait most often spoken about him by others.

Incidentally, Duran Buckler's ready entrance into agreements of using either of young Morsan Brask's two names, including Yuug Behuul, to provide himself anonymity during distribution of transmogrifiers was to forestall any risks of incrimination falling out from this current gamble, although, a lot of people knew his position was, —should misdeed or malfeasance over a patience hoping to recapture youth occur, it would be easier for him to deny his involvement, after all, his birth certificate included neither Yuug Behuul nor Morsan Brask anywhere on it.

Associates with biased understanding of his motives, or at least, those perceiving circumstances to be definitively such, entertained misgivings over his mind's general well being, —thus—talk of him being a gambler prevailed.

He also knew his sudden physical alterations resulting from his experience in Yuug Behuul's dome, which duly transformed from an eighty-seven-year-old man to a person no more than thirty, was enough to earn such title. His folks—just as elderly, at times pondered over his constant trepidations or suspicions of events bottoming out at some point, in such open manner, —if considering he was a living example of reversal in fortunes Yuug Behuul's great dome could bring one, none after encountering him could ever accept he was a day beyond his late twenties.

Diverse thought also crossed minds of citizens opportuned to

witness him talk about absence of any secrets in Duran Buckler's, as well as Mr. Brask's heart, but especially everyone's champion's, Yuug Behuul's, over any necessary information or knowledge about any subject matter concerning his son's transmogrification process he should have, perhaps, possessed, —but was refusing to disclose, a situation their respective peers took a lot of pains to suggest to both men at every opportunity, could come a-haunting much later. *'Then why so many worries witnessed of both of you—-?'* —some wanted to know, *'—if there wasn't anything to hide.'*

When asked, young Yuug Behuul admitted his grandmother—since enjoying many benefits of transmogrification, chief amongst which was now a renewed youth. He said jokes about how a long list of men in his father's brotherhood could no longer recognize her to be their friends kindly mother they often met whenever one reason or another brought them over to Redwood mansion, but a young assistant, a younger sister whom they hadn't met, or maybe a new wife.

Each time allusions to spouse hood were made of his grandma, Yuug Behuul's would ponder a little over why his grand father allowed his patience betray him shortly before his time was due to pass: he'd passed only hours before such an important discovery broke surface. With hindsight, he—Yuug Behuul envisaged a world of difference, an alternate outcome in which his grandfather lived on had he waited just a day longer, —because soon afterwards, a visiting nurse discovered his lifeless frame on his bed only a few short hours his end came robbing him any chances taking advantage of a life restoring procedure: a synonymous outcome for him as had been for everyone of his peers had been certain, though, Yuggy did on one occasion opine neither he nor his father were conversant with, nor possessed even a faint idea how useful their discovery—which in itself appears terrifying was gearing to be, for people in his granddad's situation—hence even they hadn't made any extra in ensuring his was processed.

It was during one of these sessions of extended interrogatives, a most relevant question was saliently posed him,

"How's your grandma now Morsan Brask?"

"Very well, thank you---" Yuug Behuul told his interrogator promptly,

"Yuggy—" Yuggy was Yuug Behuul's other alias some of his peers sometimes referred to him by, "—I mean, how's her condition, how does she feel, how does she look, where is she now, what's she doing each morning, or each afternoon?"

"Oh, I see what you mean," intoned Yuggy, he couldn't have imagined any other reason for this journalist's question other than his grandmother's well being, or of her spirits. Of late, '*how is your grandma doing today?*' Was among some questions younger men regularly posed him about her,

"--I thought you meant her your well wishes, or asking after her feeling."

"Of course I do, but my question is, can you explain to us what she does from time to time, from day to day, if she's healthy, is she still like your grandma, you know? ---grandma you used to know?"

"Oh, I see, I see what you mean," Yuggy was trying his very best to sound mature, "--she's younger now, each morning she prepares meals for us--- according to dad, how she used to during good old days—when he was my age."

"During good old days when she was your age?"

"Yes---, no! ---I mean when 'he' not 'she', —he was my age. She also goes jogging, you know? -— when you run around town in your sneakers, tank tops, track suits or fancy shorts."Yuug Behuul replied producing a photo of a young woman he hoped to convince others was his grandmother.

"Yeah Yuugy, we all know what jogging is," replied a journalist poised to ask his own question.

When examined by journalists, it turned out to be a photograph of an image of a young female everyone in attendance unanimously agreed could not exceed twenty-two of age: blue-eyed, blonde haired, athletic looking woman in green tank tops matching a fancy red shorts.

When closely compared to a photo of her a day before undergoing transmogrification, vestibules of resemblance of Yuug Behuul to her told them she was indeed his rejuvenated grand mother described by him only moments ago.

Yuug Behuul quickly identified his dad standing beside his mother in another photo snapped just before her procedure, then identified him in another photograph three days ago—-in which foregoing's now now made appeared to have twice her age in years.

"Really, Morsan, you expect us to agree with you its your grandma on there?"

"She is, she is, —ask my dad," protested Morsan Brask brushing off cookie crumb carelessly thrown on his shirt by shaky hands, he was suddenly afraid others might have started assuming him a maker up of stories for TV networks, a trait he was aware a lot of his peers were guilty of, "—it's my grandma!" swore he an oath he hoped convinced everyone he was being truthful, "—dad, dad," protested Yuug Behuul directing his gaze towards where his father sat with other viewers, "—isn't it grandma's photo?"

From where spectators sat, a man's voice: Mr. Brask's began issuing an affirmation of his son's claims,

"She is," agreed Yuug Behuul's father, "—he's right, it's my mother, ---his grandma, Yuug Behuul, his real name Morsan is my son." More concerned with his son's progress than proceedings, Mr. Brask felt proud of his son's knack to handle himself well in public.

"Isn't grandma---grandma anymore?" Yuggy pressed on, "she seems too young to me to be grandma."

"She is, she's still your grandma—Yuugy, don't worry about it" came his father's reassurances.

Needless to say, louder gasps over unbridled innocence in Yuggy's remarks to his father, accompanied by a few bursts of laughter, spread, one wouldn't be wrong to assume a TV network where audiences are sometime given crash courses on how to react on prompts by a cue person somewhere away from a camera's view---before commencement of shows, were at it, ---although, some of these gasps could yet have been exhilaration certain twerps allowed on set failed to restrain themselves from showing for merely appearing on a TV show, ---it was never known.

Some of laughter presumed to have been induced by cues sounded shallow, ---some thought---unwarranted, but au contraire, it was instead true, none there received any signals to execute gasps higher in decibels previous to subsequent gasps when photos of elderly grandma Brask transmogrification were shown, nor were anyone ever cued to hyperventilate when a moderator exhibited her 'after' pictures for all to see. This prompted everyone including viewers at home calling in, to confidently confirm claims by Yuug Behuul or his fellows of 'young group' seated at various places on set---about instances of certain of their own folks emerging with similar results after undergoing a procedure inside their friends dome.

When inquired as to their whereabouts, a few affirmers informed their families couldn't make press appearances due to contractual agreements preventing exposure.

Yuug Behuul, his father then their investor, —faux Mr. Brask, were pleased with themselves where they nestled on set, it was their baby after all, so successes now being affirmed by strangers on TV networks represented a culmination of their efforts alone was all theirs to cherish. Like his usual self Mr. Brask was thankful for proper contract terms which he saw was effectively preventing people capable of robbing them of their celebrity or even stealing their thunder, a possibility clearly denoted by presence of their beneficiaries' friends or kin here on set steadfastly hyping them without prior permission, or giving testimonies that indicated regrets over their prevention from sharing in widely televised celebrations of an achievement originating from endeavors of others.

In generally, viewer's collective reaction to an utterly wondrous set of photos of a twenty-five old jogger—whose grandson's father, appearing a little under twice her age, publicly claimed before others was still in her nineties, —was still a victim of sexual attraction; cat calls, suggestive comments or behaviors from young men unaware she owned enough years to be their great grandmother, was well worth it.

8

A visit to save a scientist,

his inquest to America.

Constant satisfactory outcome of transmogrification procedures leading to a tremendously bettered quality of life patient's immediately assumed soon after exiting any given transmorgrifier—a lot of folks suspected came into being in some government laboratory—-but remained under wraps till future times when it's unveiling, or proper public presentation occurred through a family business, perhaps some private enterprise, was astonishing. All over, there came into being elderly folks in their twenties, their faces healed of disfiguring wrinkles usually adorning them. What astonished folks more was how alacritous a positive picture of their renewed, or renewing persons came to fore, it was usually only a few days---no more, of undergoing one's procedure, thereafter, no one could ever again hear their voices quivering each time they spoke, nor could anyone differentiate them from contemporary twenty year olds in whose ranks they'd returned to join.

It was all good how things carried on smoothly, suspicions nonetheless lingered, a lot of questions remained unanswered.

These returnees, or new young, or if referred to as 'young again's, an appellation societies all over chose to bestow on them, referred to them as, accepted them to be, or enjoined everyone they ought to be though of as, found norms, life in general, ways inherent in modern living or culture, or approaches to life by today's generation of humanity intolerably bizarre, it was different from counted as acceptable norms of their time, —better put, what passed for normal during their prime.

On countless instances, these reversed folks were caught dutifully eavesdropping into meaningful conversations in bars, lobbies, even in elevators or other places people often gathered to gossip, —to find out what opinions of them younger contemporaries held. From these conversations, they deduced viewpoints of how much change there has been in America, decide on which was an acceptable culture or not, ---to them, degradation ruled, decay compared to what obtained during their time, was rife.

Society constantly perceived how these young elders eagerly seized every available opportunity to berate truly young folks when beseeching them with impolite questions posed in such derogatory manner respondents were nearly always taken by surprise, or left lacking in spirit to counter with enough oomph capable of staving off more impoliteness or embarrassment they felt in their failure to offer an equally sassy retort, —a reaction witnesses recognized for what it was: modern younger generation's own little way of admitting disparaging titles given them may not be untruths after all: at seventy, their viewpoints remained they were no longer kids, —should not be treated or talked to as such—even by much elderly nonagenarians, or centurions now running around town looking not a day beyond their thirtieth,

'—Couldn't you kids---' their reference to 'kids' here meaning their fellow citizens, —ranging in ages anywhere from one to seventy, '---have *faired better?'*---Some of their other rhetoric's ---whether factual or false, included, '---*Ours was better during our time,*' ---or '---*What's our world coming to?*', though, more frequently, their outward show of disappointment uttered most became: '*Couldn't you kids have done things any better?*' ---This disparaging use of 'kids' in reference to them, most often occurred in conjunction with an arrogant septuagenarian's, octogenarian's, or nona-genarian's condescending address hinting on their failings.

Once transmogrification procedures commenced around locali-ties in America, ---America—like all good that's ever happened to humankind since his inception—of course was again first to enjoy whatever privileges reversal to youth brought with it.

Yuug Behuul was, —in a conversation with his pa, acquainted with how there were abound—these days, an upbeat atmospheres around everyone, he recognized fun---in many citizens pursuit of daily affairs, hope was palpably present everywhere, long-lost longings for a much better or a more certain future once again returned.

According to Yuug Behuul's recollections—when he sometimes sat idling in his room, reflections of various schools of thought in those first few months of working elders back to youth, was initially sugges-tive of—only financially well positioned to fund their procedure---or those whose children hadn't abandoned in some nursing homes, would enlist first for a procedure.

Events proved how far off mark those schools of thought were: as it turned out, those assigned honest personal nurses indifferent to embezzling whatever funds they could lay hands on from their ward's family's coffers, turned out ones to benefit most, or were premier on existing lists to undergo procedure before others.

Nevertheless, of a sudden---in Eden Wyoming appeared untold number of long forgotten, long-presumed dead, celebrities of past eras, guardians of society, of culture, commanders of military platoons, generals of past armies, leaders, president, even historic figures now conferred statuses of nullities nobody cared about or remembered anymore due to passage of time, —were now worth very little, reappeared, almost materializing from thin air—without inclusion in any lists.

Bewildered onlookers silently watched them queued patiently till each person's turn arrived, ---each making futile efforts to suppress whelming excitement brought on by an opportunity of an anticipated second youth in which they'd once again be splurging in life in no distant future. Though understandably, outward signs of trepidation some of them subconsciously exhibited was understandable, one couldn't be too trusting lest it turns out a charade whose likes none were not prepared for, or leaving them very hurt.

Such dignitaries benefited from privileges of occupying earlier positions in many lists for transformation at designated center springing up. Similar situations of favoring past patriots, were to repeat themselves later on around earth, —never was there a good endeavor America championed earthlings deemed unfit to tag along.

According to reports from Brask's investment's public relations department, mass reacquisition of youth by all sorts of people was to commence here in America first, seniors of lands elsewhere were welcome to follow later at their own convenience.

Still and all, only a few weeks after procedures commenced bringing forth most positives of results, media organizations conjunctively acting with quidnuncs in these other countries, began leveling accusations---in what could pass for charges of betrayal by a country they couldn't prove owed them sustenance, like:

*'America, what about us?', —*or, *'they don't care about us,'* or, *'Oh, I heard in America, there are no longer old people, all their elderly's are young, they don't want us anymore,'*

Befuddled listeners, sometimes few, at other times—plenty, simply shake their heads in utter disbelieve, ---none could ever fathom a society without seniors or elders amongst its citizenry. Disgusted with what supposedly were inebriated folks, would simply proceed in their pursuits of other affairs.

At other times, in these other countries, —according to what

Yuug Behuul heard on TV, some of other prevalent comments often posed in questions were,

"Did you know---" a speaker suddenly begins but halt himself only after these three words, to momentarily consider if remarks he was about making contained any veracities at all, he or she then looks from one person in his audience to another, before proceeding, "---once you enter inside America, you become young again?" ---additionally, he or she always goes on to explain away how he, she or they heard theirs: Americans', was better breeze, how their water was sweeter, all of which such gossip usually clarifies---culminated into better effects on humans. Their account of events usually end by their hinting it was what wise folks threat: America, thought almost spontaneous reversed people from old to young, ——not some strange sinister technology nobody knew or ever heard anything about prior to now.

At other times---or at places of gathering, especially of worship, people with partiality to liquor---it had been noted, ——momentarily bettered by it, or others overwhelmed by faith, suddenly delve into inconsistent utterances,

"I hear over there in America there is fountain of youth, it's a house, you have only to go inside one to come out looking like you were when you were twenty years old, it reverts you into a twenty year old---I tell you. I'm not just talking about looking it, you feel like you're twenty again, then, you begin to age again from there."

But of course, even in those parts, science establishments manned primarily by scientists with careers thriving solely on empirical evidence invariably dismissed such claims with arguments,

"Such is practically impossible, there is no known event or story of anyone once again becoming twenty years old in their nineties,"

"If you could possibly show me just one subject, a beneficiary of your contraption evidently reversed from ninety to even a day younger, I'd be willing to pay you a million pounds," constantly constituted discourteous answers to follow. Though, ---no one ever assumed such pettifoggers possessed one million pounds at their disposal to settle debts should their bet be a bad one, it nevertheless became a constant rejoinder disputants learned to employ in absence of a more cogent response.

Anyhow, on one particular occasion, when a rather contentious elder amongst his fellows in Lesotho met with proof of age reversal photos of an Idahoan it was said to him, was actually ninety---if going by dictates on his birth certificate, but appeared no more than a third of a nonagenarian's age. On peering closer, he may or may not have realized any truths about it, still he—gentleman-Lesotho very coyly resorted to a new theory of his own supposedly to save his act,

Referencing images of a person he feigned not recognizing to be more than twenty inside a rectangular picture he held in his right hand,---gentle-man from Lesotho said in a particularly forceful dialects of natives of his locality,

"Oh, you wouldn't really believe I'd believe he is ninety years old, do you?" Arguments he propounded his opponent to further support his position, was: perhaps photos of a phony twenty some odd years old masterminds hoped to pass off for a rejuvenated someone in his nineties—most probably a great-grandson, all being to facilitate an extortion of his one million pound he has yet to win.

By way of expressing a suspicion, he suggested several reasons he pictured in what he held in his hand could never be procured for a thorough scientific examination which must of course include a DNA test to establish if claims about his advancement in years: a ninety-five year old, contained any truths, —not some persnickety twenty-five old photographically altered perhaps to ensure there were no incriminating proof of fraud, or to offer a remote resemblance to an elderly Idahoan whom to all intents or purposes was someone neck deep in an on going plot to deceive others in scams they all hoped could not be uncovered.

Encouraged by thoughts of an approaching jackpot soon to be won from an adversarial side whose one million pounds he learned was ready should they lose to him, he fierily argued before a local betting organization charged with registration of betting participants, to allow him present a ninety-five-year-old from somewhere else---his proof of a nonagenarian's general semblances looked like, furthermore, a person none of them ever met before or knew---to serve their process as proof subject. Such person must agree to a DNA test to verify age, at a laboratory only he knew. DNA test conducted must then again be repeated at some other laboratory of his choosing at a secret location organizations in charge must allow him visit unaccompanied, before onward transportation of his test subject to America for transmogrification procedure. He warned his one million pounds had to be made readily available for his collection once it was all over, —because, he hoped to avoid being infuriated, or having to do same to others later on. Scientist Schilling also let them know employment of unrelenting barristers to represent his interest in a breach of contract suit certain to be instituted against them for everything they owned, was now a top priority of his.

It was arranged thus for him a week before news of betting between people in far off lands coupled with threats by an impatient scientist promising he afterwards intended to waste no time, —in granting audience to tattle tales propounding furious lies over a machine

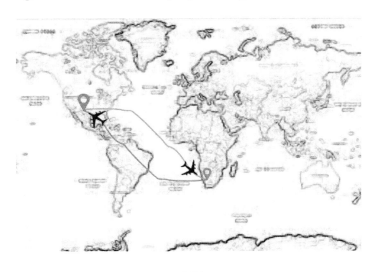

capable of making old men, young, wrinkled grannies---belles again in America, once his point was proven, —was forwarded to Yuug Behuul's gang by CNN once it reached America.

It saddened humankind elsewhere to learn in spite of western video footages providing concrete evidence, their countries continued dragging their feet in jumping onto a scientific band wagon.

To ensure a wide dissemination of news regarding a timely advent of Yuug Behuul's fountain of youth, each member of Americas young gang signed on to sponsorships by fundraising organizing committees were detailed to various parts of planet earth to spread information about.

Together with appointed enablers, Yuug Behuul jetted off to South Africa republic in whose vicinity dust ridden Lesotho is encircled. It was where a naturally argumentative Scientist Jon Shilling, a religious fanatic who never accepted what everyone else viewed once, recognized it for what it was, or found needless to argue against, a non conformist, —popular for his in depth analysis of everything, resided.

A couple of days before expiration of time allowed to withdraw himself from betting, a sympathetic Yuug Behuul Brask, made one more attempt to stage an intervention to at least help save him from an impending loss of a million pounds should he have stashed such amounts away in some bank account, or massive debts if ha hadn't.

In further attempts to save scientist Schilling from losing a fortune, little Yuug Behuul---empowered with information—an insurer in addition to a wealthy industrialist syndicating his businesses with their whole affair, was willing to bankroll entire trips like this, not just stopping at offering a handsome check to anyone disposed to accompanying him to a rendezvous with a scientific citizen of elsewhere, saw no reason to relent.

He solicited travel companionship from Nathar Saller's transmogrified grandmother for this particular trip, she was just what they needed to prove their claim to dubious scientist Schilling in Africa's horn to prove a fact. Explaining how his own grandmother failed to see any reason to accompany them on a needless trip—saying exasperatedly; 'it *works, cant they just take a look at me, they ought to be here see for themselves?*

Yuug Behuul somehow managed to secure an agreement with his peer's relative after an offer of a bigger paycheck was communicated to her.

Early morning of second of June 2022, —just after sunrise, visitors in a nondescript European Peugeot 404 sedan, turned up at Jon Schilling's home he more often than not made an ad hoc laboratory out of when necessary, bringing with it Yuug Behuul's traveling team. Before long, Nathar Saller's rejuvenated family alighted, followed by Nathar himself, then Yuug Behuul.

Moments after familiarizations ended, Yuug Behuul—now emboldened in his trip leadership proceeded to identify his colleague's grandmother to Jon Schilling as, ---what Jon Schilling -'*could never believe were true, a lady in her nineties*', urging him to back of an out of any bets at once or risk losing it for sure. Yuug Behuul in his childish way, attempted to convince Schilling erring as he was, their reason for visiting was to save him from making unnecessary payments—if at all he possessed a million pounds, or from debt---if he lacked such funds to pay up in an eventual loss, pointing out it was he, his father, his friend Nathar---there with him, among other avowers—authorities in American hired to prove to everyone transmogrification procedure, or technology, did in fact exist, he also informed Mr. Schilling it was his little group actually advancing ideas of transmogrifying earth's entire population: of seniors or elders, —depending on what designation they were known by in diverse localities, to give aged people everywhere another chance at fulfillment in endeavors in which they may have faltered in their extinct youth.

Seeing he was too far along in his quest for a quick million pounds for any entreaties from anybody—especially a young child like himself to possibly bring about a change of heart in Jon Schilling, Yuug Behuul capped off his adjuration by telling him their undertaking to warn him was so they: he, his buddies, perhaps their parents, could maintain consciences free of guilt by living up to their responsibilities of taking any necessary action to help forestall costly errors by doubtful people such as he was.

Yuug Behuul last appeal to this Dutch expatriate before their failed expedition departed, was,

"It is true, mister, it is true, —but in any case, should you fail, we will see what we can do for you in America."

When scientist Jon Schilling still continued to refuse budging, —visions of all a million pounds could do for him, not least, equipping of his laboratory with up to date scientific gadgets he needed for his scientific experiments—since caused a sensory malfunction, compelling him to stand his ground.

Without further choice, Americans convinced their good Samaritan's job was done, but knowing a second chance to meet Mr. Schilling for a final showdown, was nigh, departed with Mr. Brask expertly chauffeuring their rented old rickety jalopy away to what turned out to be a tourist destination of little importance to them, secretly marveling at his son's ruthless efficiency at conveying information to others.

Scientist Schilling's wish granted, authorities in his locality: comprising of corrupt indigenes hoping to make quick financial gains regardless of which side came out tops in any disputes, —even a bet such as was on, provided necessary funds to Mr. Schilling to procure himself an elderly person from any of Lesotho's region of his choosing.

One ninety-nine-year-old friend of his', a petty farmer—convinced obstinacy was not a trait he shared with his friend Mr. Schilling, volunteered himself knowing all there were left for him on earth was but a little time, perhaps only a matter of days, —maybe not, or weeks, —again, maybe not, or months---or if were lucky enough, even a year or two—then this life ends for him, —except by some stroke of luck—placing him amongst a lucky few genetically predisposed to live longer: —quite a few stories of folks living beyond a hundred in his parts were abound, moreover, he detested thoughts of suddenly passing if life could ever continue regardless of how shriveled with age he becomes, living on for everyone—including himself was a better choice or option. Sadly—to him, there were such overwhelming odds against such phenomena, —no one in history could ever boast of living on simply because he wished it, a time must always come when everyone bows out, for him it was no longer going to be a long time from now, he expected it to be soon than later, however, if stories about transmogrification in America represented a silver lining often talked about for him, America, here he comes for his own once in a lifetime opportunity found only there.

For thirty pounds offered him for his involvement, farmer Tutu, on an appointed date, gladly extended his wrinkled dark arm to a phlebotomist retained to facilitate their operations, to have blood drawn for DNA tests. Before an hour passed, verification were in, farmer Tutu was indeed ninety-six years old – not a day less. To further verify his' was a proper test subject, he took samples of farmer Tutu's blood to another laboratory not specified to organizers to greatly reduce their chances or power to influence results of tests thereby forcing him make a one million pounds payment.

Errant driver of a dilapidated taxi conveyed him to his destination in search of another secret laboratory to conduct a second test. Chauffeuring rather dangerously, he grew nervous when snugly nestled on his seat, his passenger: scientist Schilling just wouldn't stop throwing furtive nervous glances behind him, as they sped along unpaved dusty roads, it was imperative he find out soon enough if any car, or cars were on their tail.

At one point his passenger even suggested if there was any way he could spin his taxi's rear wheels to cause an upward billowing of plumes of dust onlookers would later testify to policemen, —potentially obscured their views as well as views of any car possibly tailing them covertly, poor fellow, it was his attempt at verifying he was not being followed by some Secret Service personnel looking to track him down to whatever secret laboratory chosen for a probable influencing of

YUUG BEHUUL AND THE FOUNTAIN OF YOUTH

outcomes of tests to effect a victory for his betting adversaries thus rendering him one unlucky fellow of a lot while everyone else earned lucky cash.

Following a generous cash tip to induce cooperation, Schilling's errant driver abided by instructions, —giving it all his might, soon, what comprised their entire speedy trip along dusty highways, bush tracks or pot hole ridden trails, all of which must first be navigated before reaching their destination, were a series of sudden slowing downs, followed in quick succession by rapid acceleration calculated to cause his taxi's rear wheels to spin with rapid revolution raising plumes of an all important dust upwards to cloud surrounding air, —successfully shrouding them from view, then, they'd speed off into distance with a great deal of velocity to ensure none could determine their direction.

Convinced there were no tails on him, Jon Schilling was dropped off at a junction where he commenced crisscrossing roads, streets, pathways, generally zigzagging his way around in a nondescript village--in his final effort to lose any spy detailed to follow him about on foot. He finally stole into a small featureless building housing a small laboratory licensed to conduct such tests for villagers. Not long afterwards, results obtained was in complete corroboration with his other test result already in his possession,

"Whoever this test subject here is---" began his fellow scientist manning Lesotho's most secret laboratory, "---couldn't be below ninety-six years old, maybe more, but not less, ninety-six at least."
Jon Schilling nodded his head, he was on track to become a proud owner of what nothing on earth could prevent him from winning.

Proof of his patient, —or test subject's, – or a guinea pig's, —call it whatever's—age, now verified by proper DNA tests, he waited to see how their clandestine plot to convert his—ninety-six-year-old man shriveled up after decades of drudgery, into a youngster whose appearance could fool people was in his mid-twenties—with their transmogrifier, he sassed.

Exactly half an hour after his option to drop out from betting expired ---which was two days after his American visitors departed, officials of a Lesotho regional government charged with overseeing betting organizations, arrived his home laboratory to officially inform him his option of removing himself from bets was irreversibly lost. Same official made it clear enough to him if he chose to do so then— even at half an hour past regulation time allowed for withdrawals, he must according to applicable laws, still have to pay one million pounds to his adversaries.

He showed them his door declaring intentions of quitting couldn't cross his mind even if he tried to make it, bragging he was in it for good – till findings are clear---come what may. He made a point in letting them know they needed to make certain his one million pounds was kept waiting for him in a bank account, warning —as he had already hired a barrister in preparation of commencing a threatened civil litigation nothing could cause a termination of, or withdrawal from—no matter what actions they commenced, what threats they uttered, or how sincerely they ended up pleading with him to relent or forgive a million dollar debt owed him, was going to be an impossibility —-till he was paid his dues. To affirm his resolution, he reiterated his withdrawal would never happen.

Ignoring his threats to litigate, Lesothoan's obliged with to it's regions government's official business, departed his home laboratory for events to proceed as expected.

To see their side's process to completion, farmer Tutu accompanied scientists Jon Schilling to United States very own embassy where they obtained visas to America, thereafter, embarked on a journey.

After a week vacationing, Yuug Behuul, his father, Nathar Saller with his folks in close tow boarded an aircraft which was also bringing with it from Lesotho, —but without any of America's most benevolent citizens knowing, Jon Schilling farmer Tutu along with resident Dutch colonialists—many of whom also hailed from other municipalities in South Africa republic, they numbered no less than thirty. Their billing was to testify before press people much later, en route to America

Mr. Shilling, —himself an eighty-six year old man became accustomed to musing to himself—in which he would secretly wish it all contained an aorta of truth in it: '—*there was nothing wrong in being young again*---' Still, he was convinced he was about to come into one million pounds of which elderly farmer Tutu—for allowing himself become his test's guinea pig, was guaranteed a sultry twenty thousand pounds regardless of outcomes of their quest to America, for transporting an aged Lesotho person to a foreign jurisdiction abroad to be put through rigors of a scientific test with undetermined effects on human body.

All involved opted to legally equip themselves; Schilling hired his one attorney, Lesotho betting organizations—secured four, farmer Tutu held on fast to one he could find—a long time friend. Six remaining lawyers represented others Lesotho betting agency managed to coerce into raising a hefty one million pounds in contention.

Everyone eagerly awaited whatever profits their investments was bound to, or at least, promised to make them should in case their side came tops.

9

How a lost bet,
proved it all.

Off to Big Sur California they went once United's rickety Boeing 717 aircraft ferrying them back to America landed in JFK New York City after making twelve stops on remote islands, one an emergency to fix a spark plug, —where visiting Africans and Europeans first snapped photographs of really tall buildings to keep as souvenirs before recommencing their journey, they were saddened on their return to JFK to find two of three planes slated to travel to California had departed, leaving behind Jet Blue's aircraft departing twenty hours hence.

In about five hours or six, after take off twenty four hours later, another of Boeing 's plane, a 787 came wheels down on LAX where waiting Sikorsky helicopters immediately took off with all thirty inquisitors in them.

For Mr. Morsan Brask, it was opportunity he needed to create utter awareness of his son's fountain of Youth come to him on platter of gold—a terminology he reserved his choice to use as he pleased, presenting itself in such grand manner, —however, circumstances surrounding this new opportunity of processing visitors from afar began suffering almost at once.

There became a great many instances of long shadows of doubts cast over it, a situation seemingly multiplying more in days prior to their visit to Africa, especially elsewhere on a planet so ill equipped to make head or tail of indecipherable bits of stories about a 'youth-giving' invention reaching them from America—that was now attracting foreigners.

Yuug Behuul's instrument became for Duran Buckler, his life's second of two most important investments---or, more succinctly put, one of only two throughout his days, —a second since that fateful day a long time ago when his ma bought him a lottery ticket, he placed into his piggy bank he spent many a long moments on numerous occasions welcoming back to him each time it got lost, or when he gave it away, or when he tossed it away, those series of events causing him a failure to redeem it for six decades—instilled in him, a remorse that had now left him poised to deal in this particular case alacritously, ---what later on in his own retrospect, equaled efforts he made in erasing taunting memories of how much time was lost, or he wasted over redeeming his billion dollar ticket.

At Redwood, huge pivot front door opened on their approach to reveal a sort of lush interiors no expatriate arriving from Africa or Europe—perhaps elsewhere ever set eyes on. They were quickly ushered towards Redwood's North East wing where they came upon a tall mysterious structure made of what appeared to be glass, --- but learned later-on was a kind of crystal they could see through. At various parts of it were couplings with some other shimmering material whose identification first required a series of experiments.

All around it's bottom's circumference where they stood ogling at it with an almost childlike wide-eyed delight, steam perhaps a kind of electronic aura coursed lightly around, rising about eight floors high.

"Welcome to my house Mr.---" —began Yuug Behuul's father outwardly pleased events where unfolding according to his liking, "---please—kindly follow me, this way—"

Silently, his team of attendants tagged by his recently arrived visitors, followed him into an adjoining room where a staff diligently entered old farmer Tutu's name into a registry of, what to Tutu himself, must have been a register of names of people previously processed through whatever they'd just seen was before now, hence his name was entered at it's lowest vacant line.

"I'm curious about these people listed here?" —he ventured to ask,

"Don't worry about a thing, they are good folks, each one of them are young again's, —beneficiaries, after undergoing what you are about to go through—themselves, look how happy they all are now."

These assurances almost sounded like one or another of many lies spreading around, or some of those gimmicks intended to fool him, scientist Jon Schilling scoffed; *'he'd seen such before'* —his scoff meant, he wouldn't let mere remarks fool nor deter him from what to him was gearing up to be an easy win. Regardless of what capabilities what they'd just seen was touted to possess, regardless of how ominous it appeared, there just wasn't anyhow his ninety six year old subject accompanying him here for a verifying procedure could suddenly reverse to being twenty four years of age, an impossibility that transcended every known law in science, still, a nagging feeling of how wonderful it would be—were it true, lingered somewhere in his heart.

Registration done, old farmer Tutu limped along with others to where Yuug Behuul's dome he later on during joyous celebrations, dubbed; world's best *gift, a lifesaver,* ---even though it was yet to save his, life's *best thing to ever happen to anyone*---which he secretly prayed his creator to make sure included him in due course, *fountain of youth, be it all for old-men, 'couldn't similar technologies have come along ever since, look how many people have died of age?',* '*Oh-my-word!'*, stood imposingly as an electronic hum resonated concurrently with what appeared to be tiny electric sparks continually exiting all around it's side.

A quick tutorial from Morsan Brask prepared him:

"Mr. Tutu---," said Mr. Brask to him,

"Farmer Tutu," he was quickly corrected, "farmer Tutu, I have farmed all my life, therefore farmer I must be called, farmer you must refer to me at all times,"he stressed.

"All right, farmer Tutu," agreed Mr. Brask, "---farmer Tutu, once you go inside it, you are going to stand in it's middle, say these words thrice--" Mr. Brask proceeded to tell farmer Tutu what's to his volunteering expatriate European residing in a part of earth where similarities were abound, with an African alias, what appeared to be some sort of incantation.

For farmer Tutu, they were fine words, accepting an instruction to utter them was perfectly alright, he knew he hadn't much choice anyhow, there was no use in reneging after coming this far to America, '*what use is it retracing my step---when it mattered most because of mere words a host instructed me to utter---'* thought he. Words were merely words that could neither demean nor belittle, moreover, he was a faithful conversant with Christian incantations, thus, his sensible considerations of these two factors elicited a quick agreement from him.

Preparing to venture inside, he chipped in a quick comment on how frightful it suddenly appeared to him,

"It is frightening," said he, his voice suggesting a terrified state of mind, ---it quivered speaking those words. Farmer Tutu found himself hoping spectator's failure to stop him was due to a misobservance of his fears, otherwise, reaching forward to prevent him from proceeding by way of uttering discouraging words would have been appropriate, instead,

"Are you sure Mr. Tutu?", —someone inquired, suddenly not sure about it all,

"You are certain I won't be harmed—ey?" —inquired he.

Tutu's sudden reaction of doubt oppositely elicited what was hoped for, everyone there howled in some nervous laughter that failed to elevate anyone's moods.

Indeed, it made sense to them too, transmogrifiers—a contrivance—one of which was ominously bearing down, was scary to gaze upon, let alone venturing inside it, only bravery or a total absence of caution has been one of only two known impetuses to embolden anyone to attempt anything half frightening as it.

Albeit their reluctance, amongst them in attendance were a few determined---but even they afterwards admitted openly, —except a matter of their life, an impending death, or horrendous torture, nothing on earth—not even for a death wish would suffice to convince them a venture inside it—notwithstanding what it was purported to do for one. A few present disclosed their attempting it would entirely dependent on whether someone else present: ---meaning farmer Tutu, whose valorous approach towards it, —hopefully succeeded by a subsequent victorious reemergence from it—still intact, —that they stood there patiently awaiting his next moves, first tried it.

Morsan Brask sensing an imminent shattering of what remained of farmer Tutu's courage, intervened,

"Not to worry mister, um, farmer Tutu," —said he to Tutu, taking him aside, they conversed in a low tone that was somewhat difficult to hear from where others stood.

Scientist Jon Schilling continued in his silence, for a while now one activity noticed about him was his silent observation of proceedings, —making notes as he did so, his one million pounds he believed was a fore gone conclusion, not far away from his mind.

Inarguably, large sums of money in his account at a financial institution comforted him enormously, it elicited an only smile since arriving from him, Yuug Behuul's transmogrifier—he'd learned it was called in these parts, appearing so ominous almost convinced him it could achieve what reports ceaselessly propounded about it everywhere, still, he couldn't shake troubling suspicions organizers away from sight, were doing everything within their power to further fool him along with every other pundit, from his mind. He wasn't going to have what he knew was a plot to undo him, like him, none about agreed it possessed any real powers to sooner or later make his farmer young, thus presumed a manifestation of truths about transmogrification was nigh. He relaxed to wait some more.

Scientist Schilling was a clever man, whilst making plans over his impending wealth or winnings—should his position prevail, he also provided himself a contingency protocol of subsequent actions were a different outcome to result, —including if his adversaries somehow managed to eke out a win---which, —even if considering there were no precedents for such never before seen instrument, still demonstrated foolishness for anyone to rule it could never perform as claimed, ---though, none present could boast a memory of ever seeing a comparable creation before, let alone been inside one like it, —but given boundless technological advances made possible by science in recent years, nothing, nothing at all ever surprised anyone anymore, only Yuug Behuul's transmorgrifier—if it were true it accomplished legendary feats of reversing an old-man to a youth, told about it, would have. In any case, he knew what to do.

Aside from his house which often became a laboratory when he needed it to, —which summed up to a little over seventy thousand pounds sterling; an exorbitant amount in those parts, —into which his entire estate's value: comprising his land, his home, then his laboratory stood was factored, amounted to all his worldly possession, he owned nothing else. Jon Schilling constant financial wanting deprived him of any one million pounds with which he could pay his debts should he lose, his staking his laboratory he often boasted to associates was an ultramodern research house equipped with up-to-date instruments---a statement of which to some extent was true except---most of those scientific equipment were loans given him by Netherlands government's national laboratory. His involvement with Dutch authorities known to be ever willing to hand him all kinds of permits to have access to their equipment for lease, hire or rent for use in his private laboratory when needed, imparted artificial values presumed to amount to two million dollars on his little science enterprise.

Laxity on Lesotho's betting organization, or their failure to conduct a thorough investigation to determine ownership of scientific instruments in Mr. Schilling's laboratory also contributed to his fraudulent deception. One visit alone, a day after betting received its permit, to take stock of his laboratory equipment, then estimate their value, was all it took them to surmising they were worth well over two million pounds in value, —which was certifiably correct, —they were worth more than was required to recoup any debts owed them should Mr. Schilling tank in his bid, —seizure of every laboratory work stations found in his laboratory, auctioning them off one item after another would be adequate to recover their money, even make more cash for their effort's worth, —it was a negligence on their part already in favor of Jon Schillings who never owned any of those laboratory equipments staked as collateral asset that qualified him for considerations.

Envisaging disheartening circumstances sure to follow should outcomes not augur well, a sullen Jon Schilling called Mr. Brask to a corner whereupon they immersed themselves in a spirited conversation for five minutes, each trying to drive home a point his listener must accept: in Mr. Schilling's point of view, for Brask to please—oh—please, promise him there were no foul plays involved---or, do him a gentlemanly deed of informing him they hadn't any smart devices capable of capturing images of a doppelganger of his test subject Mr. Tutu---with them when last his crew visited his laboratory in Lesotho, with which they hoped to prepare a phony individual to emerge from inside his son's transmogrifier---to impersonate farmer Tutu, —causing him a bad loss in a bet on which his whole life now depended.

Mr. Brask, found Schillings approach to dealing unacceptable therefore hinted his position across to him in no uncertain terms how he expected all parties involved made aware neither he nor any authorities representing his family's interest in any way encouraged him into betting, thus owed him no responsibilities in partly absorbing any costs whatsoever he may yet incur from using their device which to every foreseeable intent—was still in its trial phases, he even expressed his dismay at Mr. Schilling's possessing some audacity to presume him to be no better than a common criminal willing to do whatever for a mere pittance a million pounds he had set himself at risk for, was to him.

Mr. Brask's enunciations just before both returned farmer Tutu gave Scientist Schilling hope, or strength he thought he needed to advance, it was still a test device anyhow—like Mr. Brask said, all things considered, they too could neither bet their top nor bottom dollar on a constant satisfactory outcome each time just yet. Unfortunate—Mr. Schilling, his', —would have been a changed heart were he familiar with even a word of Mr. Brask's assurances to his test subject during their conversation; 'everything will be okay', or, 'I too have been through it, look how it procedure helped reverse me back to youth,' or, '—look, I'm not twenty-five or thirty, I'm eighty-five years old—almost as old as you are, —look how young I am?' Mr Buckler presently wondered aloud if Mr. Tutu failed to see how young he seemed, '—like your own very self,' reiterated he, 'I'm eighty-seven-years-old," ---he said additionally just before calling Redwood's owner apart for a chat.

Words Buckler exchanged with Brask in their brief conversation contained a clear picture Schillings needed to have to know he was only gearing up for a loss, sadly, a sizable distance prevented anything word spoken from reaching him where he stood.

Presently, one of two assistants slowly nudged Mr. Tutu towards what until a moment ago represented; world's best gift, world's most wonderful thing to happen to any old person, a be it all, etc, etc, to him.

Relying solely on little mercies from his maker, he entered into Redwood's gigantic contrivance whereupon he followed procedural instructions as it was given him—-equipped only with his hopes for best outcomes.

Moments later when whelming trepidation inside him suddenly threatened to undermine his courage to such extent—wisdom in rushing out of there in a short notice were doors open was advisable, three circular showers of light was noticed descending from his enclosures topmost part, down to enshroud his head regions first, then coasted down over his face, his neck regions, his shoulders, —his chest, his torso, his hips, his glutes, his crotch area, then his laps, his knees, ankles, his feet—freezing his every ability to move. then effervescent light spread from around his body towards it's entire inner circumference filling it with light.

Thrice these circular light showers onlookers witnessed cascade downwards envelope Mr. Tutu, pressed into him, each time with—though, a tolerable pressure, still a frightful one to Schilling's patient who was in those lingering moments, imbued with feelings of entrapment as it occurred especially because he could not perfect his escape from within it if he needed to.

Thrice gradual lowering of three circular rings of light occurred individually from atop Redwood's great dome to course through farmer Tutu's body at intervals of about nine seconds apart. Before long it was all over—-bringing farmer Tutu's transmogrification to an abrupt end. With that, silence following cessation of an operational hum accompanying each descending circular rings of light no one there could—as long as they lived, ever find words to describe, was reinstated. A release of gas issued for it's doors to open, —both pushed outward sliding apart to reveal its insides from where—-a moment later, what could have been old farmer Tutu, an elderly gentleman until less than a minute ago—-a relic in his former self, emerged, a transformed spectacle for astonished onlookers struck with disbelief.

10

Disappearance of a rejuvenated fellow.

𝒲hile Americans, assisted by European colonial authorities responsible for Lesotho via South African republic, continued their investigations on what transpired at coastal Big Sur: on one side: over a party's failure to live up to its responsibilities of providing money owed adversaries, on another, investigations were all about missing person's report or, a disappearance of a certain scientist rumored to have bet wrongly, after he'd conned an elderly gentleman into a science experiment incapable of, or may or may not have yielded expected results.

Meanwhile, procedures carried on in incremental numbers every passing day at various centers all over America with tremendous successes casting shadows over a supposedly failed Big Sur experiment involving a European, an African—-or so, plus many scientists from other countries moot.

However, suggestions some rumors if not all, contained possible fabrications designed to undermine Brask spotless family reputation, or tarnish Yuug Behuul's good image along with his dome, or, that one event in question was a sabotage of a transmogrification procedure by disgruntled staff employers erroneously assumed were loyal. Still, mistrustful citizens remained in continual want of conviction regarding Big Sur's dome's efficacy, even if more countless successes at it everywhere without a failure was all subsequent reports thereafter, mustered.

Interested citizenry willing to engage precious moments pondering over some rumors generally surmised: that a one off failure somewhere indicated a mistake in a particular process, a sole occurrence, ---that solitary occasion in which a terrible event occurs resulting in failure—maybe even a sabotage was inadequate to prohibit transmogrification, a laudable opinion forced upon them by prevalence of success stories, loud jubilations from spontaneous neighborhood 'welcome home, or -back' partying — everywhere, edgy law enforcement agencies or their agents found intolerable.

Regarding this one off failure purported to be discovered by America's side of investigations to be truly an only anomaly, people very quickly surmised relevant government's should ultimately still approve more procedures to go on.

Fountain of youth---according to its makers or manufacturers, gained a lot from appropriate regulations wholly permitting it to be registered in medical device division of FDA's registry. These regulations in question permitted that certain leeway's on matters of efficacy should of necessity be allowed medical devices to guarantee their authentication for public use, because in science, a medical test or equipment employed during clinical trials known to prove a hundred percentile score in effectiveness, or entirely without side effects, was yet to be registered anywhere on humanity's green earth, ---they reasoned: Big Sur's one off failure—if at all it did occur, should not be grounds to confound its authenticity if majority of tests were successes, therefore it should continue to be deemed proficient in its current fashion.

Activities continued throughout designated regressification centers across America, concerned citizens: children of seniors from all works of life---including wealthy people from elsewhere as Europe found themselves reduced to beggary to gain a favorable spot on queues, or have several units shipped to them. Some resorted to consigning their elderly folks into caring services of trained employees at centers after paying hefty bribes for an early position in lists of folks to be rejuvenated.

Nowhere was excitement surrounding transmogrifier's advent or discovery more pronounced than in California where citizens were visibly proud in their dealings or utterances to each other over it's emergence from one of their own residents, —claiming it mattered very little to any one of them if he did in fact hail from Eden-Wyoming. All things considered, where soever he hailed from wasn't their main point, fortunes enterprising folks with any sort of inroads into cosmetic industry figured could be made from this 'Silicone valley'—no less, sort of device mattered more, thus was too tempting for any one of them to over look. Nevertheless, they were aware pharmaceutical companies — notably Pfizer, detested fantastic ideas of elderly folks suddenly becoming young; after all majority of ailments usually resulting due to onset of old age in people were many corporation's bedrock on which their guaranteed constant earnings, perhaps profits rested, therefore, there was no telling what fate would befall their corporation or sales of everything they offered; their profit, even their reason to exist, should every elderly person revert back to youth again.

Brask operations welcomed a new member to their team: a European from Holland bound by his own solemn oath to dedicate his remaining lifetime helping elderly people reverse back to youth, profoundly promising---in his desperate pleas as he entered it for considerations, to give it all his best to help give youth back to old-men like he once was. His hasty departure from his home country soon after offering his pledge at an inopportune time of night, to reside permanently in Big Sur suited needs to raise eyebrows in his many associates known to have already begun distancing themselves from him after his failed bet, nonetheless, his personal reason for his hasty departure from his country of last residence, was not lost on his new employers.

In what every person given a chance visual of him could only assume was a man in his late twenties, was an octogenarian with serious charges of fraud, negligence of duty, not excluding 'failure to report back to authorities' for interrogation, considering each of all three charges—possibly more in weeks or months to come, could put him away for no less than ten years apiece, Robin Hegan — which he reported his name to be to his new masters, it is not known to anyone else if they were his actual names, nor did his employees want him to use them for reasons best known to them, settled into a posh California lifestyle.

For him, any prospect of mandatorily spending ten to thirty years in penitentiaries in Europe or any of its colonies was unimaginable, luckily for him, his situation in America improved his mental state transforming his general outlook astronomically, even he knew what new fruitful life lying in wait ahead of him—was contingent upon adequate use, ---damn him, he chided himself, if he couldn't make a successful use of his time in earth's only new world.

Robin Hegan's initial doubts regarding existence of any such technology, or any other similar devices anywhere on earth—be it undeclared, with potentials to make people young, became passé for him, here he was now — once again in his youth — all bubbly, healthy, if luck continually remained on his side, sprite enough to evade haunters instituted by authorities back in that other country where he was Jon Schilling.

America surprisingly felt like home to him, his comparisons greatly favored it over his former place of residence, he dreaded endurance of lengthy time in prison—he would no doubt have had to deal with, for what? —for not paying a—one million pounds lack of proper dissemination of information—entirely blamable on govern-ment's inadequacies, caused him to owe? —or was it deprivation of proper counsel brought on by lack of funds? ---still, he faulted himself for acting almost too spontaneously on his own advisement over what he now realizes to be a severe deficiency in knowledge of facts which altogether was very scare in his former parts, moreover, were there evidence---no matter how tangible, an unnatural event of suddenly reversing back to youth was a fairish instance for him to retain doubts in him—invariably forcing him to remain unwavering in his position, thus disadvantageously pitching his vote in which he ended up making a serious error in judgment in entering a bet that ultimately became a lost cause.

Or, ---really? —for him, wasn't it that proverbial blessings in disguise? — hadn't stars of heaven shone down on him with good fortune? ---hadn't showing obstinacy in a position in which certainty eluded, or entering an expensive bet in such careless a manner it transpired, ---he came to ask himself repeatedly in retrospect, led him to realization of several truths? —now, look where he was!

Mr. Brask sat with Robin Hegan in his little Redwood office discussing in low tones over coffee, —or entertaining one indistinguish-able thought constantly nagging away at their minds, —really important bits of news, ---most of which covered mainly what Americans now christened, '*new population*' —transmitting on a TV screen all day—now given way to commercials, when a knock on his offices' door sounded, cutting short each individual's train of thoughts.

There were no servants at Redwood mansion, it's owner detested making people work in his most private of environments, instead installation of all sorts of modern computerized gadgetry configured to do chores ordinarily performed by human servants dotted everywhere.

One of such electronic conveniences stood stationed in a far corner near a tall window of his office—Morsan Brask's called a holobionic hard worker, whose duties amongst many more was to carry out any chores assigned them but with a far higher degree of efficiency than any human servants could ever attain.

"Hello---" said a police officer when Redwood's huge front doors were thrust open, ---his entire body contrasting against natural fixtures gracing exteriors of Redwood: daylight, skies, firmaments just behind him.

Official insignia on his shoulder's confirmed to Mr. Brask appearing momentarily from behind Hegan he was a captain from Los Angeles police department, ---not a Big Sur official whose uniform usually read: 'Sheriff's department'.

Behind whom they would soon learn was Captain Pesto, were four other strange constables neither men were yet to encounter throughout many hectic continuations of transmogrification bustling's transpiring all day around their Big Sur mansion grounds---constables were hired to guard.

Thoughtfully speculating all five officers were investigators from an international organization, perhaps from Netherlands securities department still hunting for farmer Tutu or his master Jon Schilling, or both. They stepped forward, while Yuug Behuul peered from behind.

"How may we help you, gentlemen?" Morsan Brask began his lead in a conversation, whilst regarding them closely with suspicion, uncertain it was a methodology their investor thought law enforcement officials deserved,

"I am Detective Pesto," Captain Pesto expertly led theirs for his team,

"—I am told at our office you received visits from two men last week on inquisition about one Jon Schilling known to be missing with another one called farmer Tutu. Records show they spoke to you over a certain process we hear is all over, is it true?"

"Yes indeed, a certain John Schilling visited, —he claimed to be a scientist from Netherlands, in attendance here in America, he was accompanied by another elderly fellow, I think his name is—Tutu, Mr. Tutu, they were both here a couple of months ago---" Mr. Brask was saying, but was interrupted,

"A-ha! —have you seen either of them, have they visited here ever before, or since?" ---Inquired captain Pesto, "---they're both missing," he added. Robin Hegan's mid-twenties demeanor as he stood by Morsan Brask, mellowed a little.

"I can't really say officer, I'm mostly away from home, there's no way of identifying my visitors while I was away—I'm sure you can understand that. Anyhow, what's wrong with both men? — haven't you seen them since betting ended last time, I understand everything went according to all expectations---"

"No, we haven't---" began a companion from behind embassy officer—Hasselhorf—slickly, his thick accent convincing both men these were people from Netherlands, "---precisely our point, everything went accordingly, no one knows why Mr. Schilling is now in hiding---"

"How do you mean it?" Of course, Morsan Brask's conjecture concerning reasons or purpose of a late morning visit by law enforcement officials of another country was correct, but it wouldn't hurt to ask, ---he might yet ascertain useful information they needed to have in their arsenal to be able to prop themselves up in their hopes to continue keeping authorities at bay, he couldn't fathom how transmogrifying an old farmer — giving him back his youth through a wonderful procedure warranted paying a million pounds-even if losing a bet was associated with it—since helping an elderly person recapture youth was enough to warrant a forgiveness of debt, but instead is now is being made to pay for his good deed.

"You see, ---Mr. Schilling entered a bad bet he wound up losing, now, old farmer Tutu is missing, until we decide betting was not illegal, of decide it was not imposed on one by another, or find out both men's whereabouts, we cannot absolve him or help get his debt be forgiven---or paid off gradually, perhaps---," Hasselhorf explained sympathetically, how seizure of Mr. Schilling's home laboratory in lieu of payment, or at least as part of it, has become an only option for sponsors both betting sides dealt with. He hinted how necessary discovering Mr. Tutu's whereabouts was, as his family's peace of mind over his disappearance was of paramount importance to Netherlands. It was Pesto's apathetic warning—he was sure both Redwood's occupants understood how important disclosing their hideout if they knew, or knew something about direness of potential consequences of failing to do so, they remembered longer with regarding their visit.

Morsan Brask understood, it could never please anyone to learn a family's disappearance—resulted from a simple error in judgment of entering into a bet he ultimately wound up losing, forcing him to take his subject with him to unknown places.

"Yes, we understand you perfectly officer, if anything, ---once we see them or learn where their whereabouts are, we're sure to let you know---" Soon after casting glances in every direction, Dutch embassy officials boarded their vehicles to depart Redwood premises equipped with Mr. Brask's promises.

11

Arrival at an elder center

hopes for a younger tomorrow.

$\mathcal{A}$ll three rejuvenation associates: senior Mr. Brask, aliased Mr. Brask, then Brask---our Yuug Behuul, plus Robin Hegan---for he was now a permanent fixture in greater scheme of events, not excluding a few other people, were now increasingly seen at regular intervals at places elderly folks frequented more often than anywhere else in their lives. Chief amongst these places were nursing homes.

On every occasion of their visit to any of such places, it never failed to amaze each person how theirs was always a gracious welcome to enjoy from elderly residents welcoming them with open arms— considering many inhabitants–aged as they were, usually hadn't any clue whether any visitation by groups connoted a commencement of a process tailored towards committing them to any nearby centers. Bitter

brawling amongst themselves routinely commences as seniors struggle to reach reach forward to make a gift of themselves to be amongst ones selected.

Correspondence to media houses by a disheartened public---it was said, was rife, how once visitors---even unlikely ones, or strangers--commonly, entered designated centers, serious tussles for whom visitors should attend to first before others must itself---first occur. It was also reported that a spontaneously chorus of, "---me, me," would reach each visitor's ears---as each senior tries to out-holler others hoping his voice carried over dims caused by other voices hollering as loud as they knew how, —all in a desperate act to ensure their opportunity to reacquire youth never slipped by. Sometimes, it would be heartbreaking for visitors, they find themselves uttering solemn prayers to Most High, to allow each elder enough to time to seize this rare opportunity of a second youth to make amends for their past errors---to finally settle every pending decades-old matter with their business associates, or, so they could embark on that extensive vacation on a remote white sandy shore they'd always seen in their fantasies, or, finally finish their effort of painting a house abandoned midway–through–thirty odd years ago---they had hitherto refused to pass on to their children, or, conclude a thriller stacked somewhere---half a lifetime ago, ---though they couldn't possibly remember exactly how long ago now, or eventually get to own a house, —travel earth , oh, that crush they once battled against, —over America's most beautiful girl in their neighborhood---spending their entire first youth dreaming about marrying her someday, —so they could finally make her theirs, ---hopefully, she hadn't aged a day since.

Yuug Behuul especially always saw on one or two occasions he accompanied his corporate associates there, undying dreams in their eyes of one day owning a great big Cadillac, start their own Corporation--that would one day rival GE or Disney. In those moments seniors reached out to welcome them—as they arrived, he would hear their promises to be nice to people this time—if given another chance. It always stirred up bitter emotions in him how some people he arrived such places sometime sat themselves down to weep, it sometime made him cry too. It was here, wasn't it? —transmorgrifier, soon, they'd all be having fun in Acapulco, fun in Disney world, fun in Las Vegas casinos---if only they could exercise enough patience to write their names on Brask Rejuvenation Ctr. Corporation's list, maybe, just maybe—they'd get to have some fun under a midday sun, hit bars like they used to, maybe move to a fine city---meet someone wonderful, make him, or if a female—her, theirs, they could move to their countryside, settle down to promenade underneath each night's moonlit skies—counting stars until break of dawn, maybe they'd do things they hadn't courage to do during hay days of their first youth: like rekindling with long lost family if apologies to each of them for all past shortcomings or for their error then of falling short of expectations would suffice to make amends. They'd ask for their forgiveness, start all over again by holding each one of them close—never letting go, —if only they could exercise just a teeny bit more patience to write their names down, then they'd be good to go. Yuug Behuul knew there was nothing these seniors wouldn't give—for an all elusive second chance at life, or, take advantage of all there were to make youth's transient beauty last them in their second youth, as many centuries as his transmorgrifier promised, —nothing.

These regrets he knew, was what compelled these inmates to cry even louder to be heard each time,

"Me, me, oh---me," Oceanfront City's nursing home seniors were at it again, jostling each other for attention of visitors arriving momentarily with outstretched arms to grab onto what to them was 'lifesaving breath', a second chance, their team's arrival foreboded.

None amongst these animated elders understood why—any visitor as those approaching currently—none of them could say for sure were involved with any center involved youth restoration business staff of their residence not only informed them, but also confirmed to them during a previous visit was now in it's final stages of approval—promising to enlist each of them in due course, chose a rainy day to visit. Still, it satisfied them to make one more go at attaining youth if only by reaching out to total strangers, who knows? ---These men might just be it, folks from 'there': their new endearing name for rejuvenation centers, *'there'*.

"Settle down, settle down---gentlemen, we will attend to every-one of you presently," announced Brask team's most relevant person to clamoring seniors, ---it was all too apparent---how he swaggered---he was beside himself with glee to realize his instructions to Oceanfront City's nursing home's management during their visit a day or two ago---to avoid intimating inmates lest there ensue a rush---such as was actualizing, ---so as to allow for a discrete selection of every eligible, or most suitable or more qualified candidates to be put foremost in line to have their much deserved second chance at youth without disturbing all other with knowledge of it, was met with ignominy, though, it didn't hurt at all to be treated like a celebrity.

His attempts to calm rowdy seniors fell on deaf ears, at their age, patience, ---of all humanly attributes or virtues was to be least expected of them, or they cared about for any one in their condition, ---given Yuug Behuul's youth device's sudden bursting into people's awareness.

Each feared exit from life lurked, patience couldn't possibly be a distinction any of them possessed anymore, ---an attributes they weren't going to have! ---especially after being made to understand 'exiting' was no longer an unavoidable part in an elder's scheme of things---if he or she simply wished to continue living, more so, they had also learned 'exiting' could now be factored out of one's existence by a mere passage through a 'big thing' called transmogrifier installed at centers across America by one Yuug Behuul, a young child they learned was yet to attain his teenage years.

True to expectations, or suspicions, perhaps trepidation, ---in those such feelings manifested, Brask Rejuvenation Ctr. Corp. team accompanied by Hegan---considering his profession's relevance to de-termining age, then verifying it later on when appearances differed, ---as well as others accompanying them, ---Fedora, a now youthful Lesotho-an test subject of Mr. Hegan's---noticeably eagerly leading them into

Ocean Front's premises, their business today—all things considered, hinged on an agreement with Ocean Front's management to grant permit to cart a select few: ones nearest exiting, off to an established places of rebirth now proliferating everywhere for their youths to be given back to them once again, for impatient earthlings to see these seniors become young enough to fulfil promises of righting those past errors in their previous youths with a second one.

12

Nagging voices of entitled folks.

$\mathcal{M}$eanwhile, time progressed without incident—encouraging every participant in blossoming ventures of making old folks young again to work in unison in making their enormous tasks of doing great good their ego's had charged them with, successes. Word seniors everywhere on earth could now harness a rare technology in one opportunity to address crushing disappointments of their first youth with a second one, continued spreading like nothing else had. Incessant talk of a child's unearthing of a miracle cure to old age, ---to aging, addressing issues of apathy associated with life's terminal stages along with it---continued.

Like every fad there ever was, nowhere was robbery of people of their enthusiasm to partake in any other profitable occupation worth remembering more pronounced than—-where else? — California's own foremost city, Tinseltown to be more exact.

Here, celebrated individuals infamous for being players in Hollywood's most prominent industry saw yet another opportunity to make it known—-in manners showing theirs was no less a hereditary sense of entitlement, it must be their folks to benefit first, or most, from any center's procedures, or else---.

"Dad, dad, —look who's here!" Yuug Behuul was speaking to his father from a ninth floor window on an occasion they idled about at home doing chores pertaining their budding enterprise,

"Who?" replied Mr. Brask to his young son, moving over to where he stood peering downstairs,

"Ghost-rider on bike, I saw him on TV on Monday, he wanted us to give his dad a chance to have another young future, he wants us to help make his dad proud of him. Dad, oughtn't we let him in at once, or else---"

"Or else what---Yuggy?" rejoined his father after a moment of construing his son's remarks a childish crush on a celebrity. Rising from his desk in what should have been Redwood's ninth floor were it's floors stacked on each other conventionally, he moved over to Yuugy's side to see for himself,

"---or else CBS Los Angeles wouldn't know they were here," replied Yuug Behuul quickly.

"I see what you mean…" —indeed, he understood his little one, it was a proven tact for enterprises in America's west coast to manipulate celebrities' proximity to themselves or their businesses to shed more light on corporate operations which sometimes engendered a wider acceptance of good, services, or products desperately needing pushing.

A quick peering down followed by an equally quick withdrawal of his head, ---a preemptive measure he thought necessary to take—-to prevent a missile hurled towards their visible persons by ninth floor's open window by an irate someone from downstairs suddenly finding rest on his peeking skull, moreover, peeping downstairs helped up his attention for what come next.

Shortly, they were joined by their investor permitted usage of 'Brask' as a name in all matters concerning business—to empower him with an identification with which to become a front representing their budding corporation as well ensuring undue botheration of his partners in their ownership of a discovery greedy corporate humans increasingly threatened to usurp each passing day by any means necessary, if whatever corporation or company: which of course were they here at Big Sur, charged with its general availability, failed to supply transmogrifier domes to interested franchises—immediately, was non existent.

A short while ago when information filtered through to him concerning these threats of an oncoming forceful approach, or an unrelenting attempt at a hostile acquisitions from; Pfizer, Glaxo sterling, or was it Sterling Winthrop, perhaps Eli Lily, ---he couldn't remember which, promising there was nothing they wouldn't give, nothing they wouldn't do to acquire whatever that transmogrifier was into their ownership—making it theirs---come what may---be it hail, hell or high water, it was this singular promise that caused Mr. Brask to consider employing—not just cops, but thugs, to keep an eye on over ambitious executives dynamically seeking to acquire stock options in their corporations none of them had invested in.

It increasingly came to be expected by, —and soonest for that matter, every affected person on earth, a want of a second chance at youth, ---much as was every pharmaceutical company on earth's aspiration's over a world wide ever crescendoing buzz about a wondrous thing, which to them translated to high billion-dollar earnings. For these covetous multinationals, that mysterious contrivance esoterically hidden—they heard, in a Big Sur house, amounted to a peculiar matter in existence whose origins is privy only to some, —that was capable of satisfying any corporation's greed, or want of being world's unique business entity towards whom everyone pandered to solicit—with their outstretched arms holding large sums of cash they hoped were taken from in exchange for youth.

"Yes, yes---I can see him, what's his name, what's his name? ---he asked no one in particular, emphasizing his attempt to achieve a recollection of names associable with his son's movie idol,

"His name is Actor Kage, ---his company's name, ---that tall fellow in pink striped shirt, his name is Matt, they both want their aging fathers saved, I think we should help them first, what do you say---dad?"

Before Yuug Behuul's father could offer his reply Yuug Behuul quickly added, "---through them everyone all over is sure to know what we have here in our house here is real; ---its ours here in our house---you know? ---even if those big drug companies hoping to make attempts to claim it is theirs or take it from us, won't succeed."

"Good idea Yuugy---good idea. I'm proud of how you think---son, but sometimes it's better to wait a little to find out what gives, what he has in mind, if he'll have good intentions for us afterwards, or if they're just out to use us for their own good – you know what I'm trying to say, don't you?"

"Yes dad," agreed Yuug Behuul, "---sometimes they act out or do stuff or make fights to happen, it puts them on TV screens during news hour, they get a bump in their popularity, then they make movies about it, tons of cash follow shortly afterwards."

Senior Mr. Brask was satisfied with his sons response.

A moment later, their investing partner, bored stiff in his small office out of which he couldn't get past suddenly peeping out to ogle at Yuug Behuul's transmorgrifier downstairs---that also served him as a rest place---though nowhere near his Idaho home's opulence, arrived ninth floor whereupon he approached Mr. Brask talking to Yuugy in their new position obscure to personalities downstairs, to join in on whatever conversation---he was certain was more or less over matters arising---going on.

In recent days, Mr. Buckler hired himself a petit secretary---one of his employees in some of his other corporate concerns he owned, a Jane Applebaum, charging her with giving her job her best, but also telling her to expect some good to come out of it all eventually. Miss Applebaum on her part sat tight, tackling each hectic work load assigned her desk or whatever her new job brought during her first few days working for B.R.Ctr. Corp, with strengths beyond what she was aware lay within her capacity to exert labor.

First, she familiarized herself with work routine, thereafter, from morning when she arrived work each day, till later evening when tasks assigned her was done, Jane Applebaum would busy herself compiling names of elderly citizens making heart-felt pleas for her urgent help.

Needless to say, quite a lot of requests landed her desk in those initial days at work — especially those from members of Mr. Brask's extended family too reluctant to ask favors, or make requests, but instead chose issuance of injunctions, even orders as a means to garnering her attention, claiming relations to her employers warranted them unalienable rights—not privilege, of placement in good spots, that no one—not even she should ever abrogate, otherwise there was no escaping bitter consequences of their grudge accompanied by their malice certain of those relatives warned her would never end.

In carrying out her duties, poor secretary Jane took heed of her own self advisement, after all, she too wouldn't behave any better under parallel circumstances. Quietly, she obediently performed her task according to these injunctions entered by kin of her employer without her master, or masters knowing, lest their problems of dealing with old age now resolvable by reversing to youth, become hers to every extent it was theirs.

She hunkered down, ---even though her contract lacked such authorizations, to include names of her own aged folks; one being a hundred-two, a second—ninety-seven, ---on B.R.Ctr. Corp's list of privileged candidates transmorgrifiable without hesitation or delays once they arrived Redwood mansion—whether or not there were queues.

Thus, witty secretary Jane on her volition succeeded in cleverly made shoeing-in of her elderly folks, plus many more seniors she covertly charged a handsome fee she declined to report to her bosses, calling it her own workplace benefit.

"Mr. Brask —" began B.R.Ctr. Corp's premier investor once he stopped beside them. He too had first peered down to observed an ever-increasing number of people gathering outside momentarily noting their continuing calls for someone to attend to them.

Listening more intently, he thought he heard what he recognized to be either Kage's or Matt's voice say,

"Please, please, help my dad, save my dad, my dad! — My dad! Oh please, I don't want my dad to die," — they couldn't quite tell which spoke thus, ---but it might have been actor Kage.

In essence, both men generally echoed similar sentiments, or held analogous impressions as were everyone else. Like all others, they too were there for themselves, or had brought their elderly parents to be rejuvenated, or to solicit a private procedure for an elderly family--- usually their mom or their dads---perhaps grandparents.

Jane, on inquiry by her immediate boss in a quick phone call through his flip phone, confirmed there hadn't been any supplication for an elderly brother, or a friend from anyone just yet, after which Duran Buckler noted issues had suddenly come to a head to prove such thing relatives as brothers, or friends didn't matter very much, before settling down for a conversation with his senior partner.

"Yes Mr. Buckler, what may I do for you?" ---inquired Yuug Behuul's father once his wealthy Idahoan partner had suitable comport- ed himself where he sat,

"Mr. Brask, I thought we agreed on a constant use of Brask as my name?"

"Yes, indeed, there was such agreement, but—when addressing all others, to us Brask's, you are still you, aren't you?" Yuug Behuul's father pointed out,

"Well---I am, but no longer in actual sense of my former self, look how young I am, no one could ever tell I'm eighty-five years old, I really must insist we stick to Brask, I need to be in a Brask character always to enable me stage an effective front function for B.R.Ctr. Corp," he pointed out, "---wouldn't you agree?"

"Correct," Mr. Brask offered his agreement, however, he enjoined Duran Buckler, "—but still, whenever you are with us, you'd be you, but to all others, Brask, it is what we agreed to at first, wasn't it? —when you address others about it---including for business purposes, then, you could be a Brask. I suggest we stick to our agreement—Mr. Buckler."

"All right---all right Mr. Brask---" hoping to prevent his corporate partner from growing suspicious of his motives, if it hadn't already done so, "---let it therefore be how we agreed initially," accepted entrepreneur Buckler. Duran Buckler then quickly put forward more insinuations, "---speaking of which – you raised issues about representing corporate interests or figures, we have secured what to us, should be lucrative agreements from three notable character portrayers; one portraying a cyborg, a mercenary, a third—an archaeologist – if you know characters I'm suggesting."

"Why not just say their names," riposted Mr. Brask his partner's dilly dallying left him a little annoyed, it represented some of those little idiosyncrasies one cleverly kept away from other people's awareness—if accord with them was to be established,

"---I haven't even a slight clue about any, 'cyborg', or 'mercenary', or 'archaeologists' —you speak of," pointed out Mr. Brask additionally. Assuming a pensive look, he furthered his position with an injunction to his junior partner, "---could you please explain?"

"I'll give you time to figure it out," —investor Brask smiled his response, "---anyhow, I was at Santa Cruz's nursing home we discussed a week ago with cattle drive's cowboy---yesterday, you know him, mister good one amongst three duelists, remember him? ---I can't recall his name right now but I'll let you know when I do---"

"Right, what happened to him," inquired Mr. Brask not certain if his partner could tell he knew each man's identities in his description, "I believe I know who you mean."

"I accompanied him to a nursing home entrusted with guardian-ship of one of his buddy of his on cattle trail, he couldn't recognize his ramrod boss or fellow—which ever applied anymore, I understand it's been quite a while they met last, since then Ramrod has transmogrified, effectuating his return to youth again, —he? – poor old fellow, he's still just as aged as time has made of him, —hardly remembers anyone or anything now."

"I guess they'd all have a chance at youth once more---Mr. Buck-ler"

"Right, —I signed him up, we scheduled a meeting right here days from now – not more than a week –"

"I'd like to meet them sometime, I can't quite figure which of them you're talking of, maybe when I see them, I'll remember exactly who you mean." Ulula-tions reaching upstairs from downstairs continued to grow, despite Redwood's height of ten storey's reached their ears clearly.

"Too many seniors, not enough pods---" one particularly high-pitched voice kept repeating. In all certitudes, he hoped to instigate a spontaneous chant enticing enough to make others want to join, none did.

Attempting to decipher some unrelenting rambling downstairs, both men upstairs deduced whomever it was howling downstairs either hoped upon Yuug Behuul's invention confidingly, or longed for his, or his grandfather's turn to arrive, for his second youth to commence.

Further deductions from utterances issuing from irate voices soaring upwards from below included his suppositions of being heard above extremely loud cacophonies of dozens of voices should he scream long, harder or louder than most, or it would be an encouragement for whomever was behind proliferation of Yuugy's magic matter everyone everywhere now unanimously branded 'Pod of Most High', or simply, 'fountain of youth', to ramp up fabrication of more units, make it more available immediately, —else!

What? —in their rationale to issue threats for a good cause, —they demanded of themselves downstairs, was disagreeable?

13

Yuug Behuul's contrivance
bring good to seniors.

*I*ntoxicated by excitement over turn of events, a lot of new young's, or young again's, or, ---call them whatever, found new vocations; one being to taking up positions for long minutes in front full-length mirrors ogling at their own selves in disbelief at what they'd become, another being to retrace their steps back to their roots---not merely by a trek through memory lane, but in all actualities. It became something of a rave for them to rekindle themselves with country-sides, —cities they visited in their childhood—which soever of either fancies appealed more to each individual's senses during their first youth. It was hoped an untimely demise each increasingly impatient yet unattended seniors---it was noted by all, hoped to avert by going through with it, didn't happen before it all ended. It was also succinctly noted if it were not excitement capable of undoing them before their time, over antici-pation---not least, could. But come to think of it, virtually every one of them were on cue to anyway's.

In spite of all fears, passing of time proved no elder harboring such trepidations met their demise from over anticipation or heart palpitations associated with anxiety, instead, their contemplation of a good outcome each anticipated, majored as a factor that contributed immensely to their continuing existence as they waited, ---perhaps pending whatever_final outcome was gained whenever it reached their turn.

Besides everything, legions of new young's in Michigan, Florida, Wyoming, Los Angeles, Seattle, etc, mindlessly appreciated constant qualities of surprising results continuing to be prevalent everywhere on daily basis as more of their fellows emerged back into youth.

Rejuvenants everywhere sang praises of young Yuug Behuul, pledging, ---for his sake, to put a lot of self-confessed errors in their conviction during their previous failed youths---never to be tried by them again---into consideration, ---if only reversal to youthfulness could be granted all remaining peers of theirs, to bring about an increment in hands willing to lend themselves to hard work this time around.

They began to see silver linings in this cloud hovering over them, forsooth, even they were wise enough to see it for what it really was; a chance for a chance for a new beginning heralding better tomorrows, Someone's good works, a child's---whom they heard told everyone he had their backs as they prepare to proceed. He had their backs indeed, after all, it was with his good works, howbeit he had done it, ---which they heard was without resorting to any primitive methods, ---affecting their psyches with a greater depth of satisfaction than ever before known, for finally conquering an almost peculiar condition of suddenly not being as young as one once was.

Even families of forever impoverished old folks in perpetually re

-duced circumstances since many years, —still immersed in real poverty presently, who ordinarily lacked any means of paying for this procedure, thinking it was bound to be prohibitively expensive when it is finally offered commercially by it's young creator—Yuug Behuul—it was said his name was, rumored to have built every portion of it, or, any other ultimately behind it all, agreed there were conscientious reasons to exercise extreme caution. This notion prevailed everywhere one looked since this sort of event was entirely new to everybody except purveyors of literature where fountains of youth had since been playing prominent roles in fables, fantasies, or corresponding folklore in various forms or guises.

Meanwhile, there were none knowledgeable on what anomalies it brought with it, ---ultra longevity they unanimously suspected was one, —nor could they find any expert to testify if an arsenal of nasty surprises—demonstrably latent, only to manifest after a while--perhaps long afterwards when it is finally consigned to memories of every single one of it's beneficiary: over population being a paramount culprit here, ---if considering humanity's poise to attain a forty thousand—maybe even more—years of lifetime effectively ruling out extinguishment of lives at what was once a usual frequency of less than a hundred, —dooming humans to facing unbearably long periods of drudgery to continue making ends meet, during which time, there'd be increasingly more progenies brought into life on earth to compound needs or wants for more worldly resources.

Quite a number of these eligible citizens—it was discovered, secretly hoped their on coming second youth brought with it, —a reoccurrence of remarkable legacies of a sweet dramatic past now rarely spoken of, or is now permanently consigned to records.

Filled with exhilaration deliverance from aging had arrived in every one of its essences, multitudes of them thanked heavens, even those doubtful joined in on spreading gratitude nonetheless—at least. To some, for once, science establishments had done good, or was thinking right—if solving aging as had been proved by this timely arrival of transmogrifier, was a matter since occupying a place on their to do list to make it a possibility for folks eagerly awaiting its arrival to live longer.

Yuug Behuul's entire family, his team as well as their investor were all smiles, once transmogrifiers reached every eligible person, finances of millions of well to do senior citizens was certain to constantly familiarize themselves with pockets of a lot of entrepreneurs managing licensed franchisers at centers where-ever, for purchase of youth: a rare commodity B. R. Ctrs. Corporation: their company initially offered America's aging public free of charge, then making them an incessant stream of returns from franchise fees.

In those moments of inspiration when extra strength in one is liberated, seniors hitherto reluctant to try a second youth found themselves suddenly be gingered up to go through with it, —their much younger relatives finally accepting it was their elderly one's only chance at making amends with his or her past, gives them their blessings to go ahead with it.

For all three men incentivizing it; Brask, Brask, including Buckler: a faux Brask, that all—liberating moments of inspiration constantly compelled them to go live on any available TV shows to excitedly voice promises, ---or to extol how efficient their contrivance was, boastfully arguing how betting one's bottom dollar, fortunes, live's savings —even pensions---were any put aside, was no longer an issue for anyone willing to go out on a limb. These assurances led to many more eligible or likely fellows in need of help from Yuug Behuul's youth giving fountain, to thank their lucky stars, or good or sunny heavens---whichever expression one was conversant with, —it happened during their time. Arms raised upwards in reverent salute to Most high; *"Hallelujah," they'd holler, "— time had indeed come—," they'd swear additionally, "—anyone willing to bet their top or bottom dollar along with their lives savings, or pensions, was being truthful,'* they'd sing.

When promises—many adjudged was akin — to a constantly seductive freeway – drivers intend traveling for its stunning sceneries

along smooth stretches, —but whereupon mishaps often occur without warning due to lurking dangers, —instilled in elderly viewers by these three men, fizzled out quicker than it gained entrance into their psyches—as it always does—due to that one lingering tale about a certain Dutch scientist, many a folk waited with bathed breaths.

Coincidentally, that one mysterious appliance in Big Sur's Redwood mansion, —together with hundreds of much smaller copies of it—yet just as efficient now installed in centers across America, earned B.R.Ctrs.Corp a reputation of being one last removed straw proverbial camels could claim saved their back from breaking.

This anecdotic opinion relayed conversely was younger folks general summarization each time news of an elderly person entering either a transmogrifiers or regressifiers somewhere, reemerges less than a minute later from it's insides, far younger than any contemporaneous fellow of modern times were, —or at least just as young—for still, it was hard to believe something so out of sync with nature, —reached their ears.

Reports continued to reach management of Brask NewLife, Corporation—which was also: B.R.Ctr.Corp, dutifully manned by third Mr. Brask—himself well settled into his second youth after rejuvenating from an elderly eighty-seven-year-old, to what was seemingly an age no one could ever at a glance suspect was not a twenty four-year-old, —how many already overcrowded centers continued to enroll more aspirants without any considerations if there were real chances of landing an accommodation on lists. My—oh—my! —it was often exclaimed all over, if hell ever saw chaos at any point in its history, then surely struggles for spots in lengthy queues transpiring on daily basis at these centers, must have been it's equal.

Dismayed onlookers soon realized what gave rise to unending hullabaloo's at these centers was each center's inexpensive price tag of free every one's procedure was going to be. Be that as it may, to add a penny, just another penny to their personal coffers making themselves richer than they already were, —if they were, touts resolved to devise a protocol to charge exorbitant fees for an operation entirely under another's ownership, all things considered, they readied themselves to enlist only least deserving seniors willing to pay hefty up-front fees—leaving some embattled franchisers at loss for what actions to take to make operations smooth.

In a center just off Hollywood boulevard, an old fellah dogged by a fetor of a stranger sort arrived to undergo his procedure so he could feel life was anew, sadly, when last he bathed himself, was an occasion occurring ages ago, his advanced years being a determinant factor why he wouldn't go anywhere near water. Anyhow, his fouling of that center's dome's interiors momentarily halted proceedings. Consequently another old fellow found himself thrust into bitter complaints of how, —if such stench accompanied transmogrification procedures, it wasn't worth it for him. Another taking cue, angrily declared if such obtained everywhere, then perhaps, dying accompanied by a solemn laying to rest might yet be a better option for him or all others in his conditions rather than inhaling such offensive fetidness from a fellow.

It took several extra curricula efforts stretching over many hours before any hopes of work progressing returned. Four, maybe five hours intervened before Yuug Behuul, —as seen on America's TV's as trans-morgrifier's inventor, whom a keen fellow at that center urgently pleaded with in sorrowful message over a smart phone communication for his immediate appearance if proceedings were to resume, arrived.

Yuug Behuul did arrive a bit too quickly stirring suspicion his folks in their crookedness may have instigated it, thus were waiting nearby to enable a quick dispatch of transmogrifier kid soon after an urgent summons, a perfect reputation or a picture of readiness gained from such alacritous show of readiness capable of making of them look good in their supposed want to cater to senior citizen's needs, was most certainly a desiration of theirs, —everyone knew.

He pranced back then forth—exactly how he observed that senior at loss for whether it was he who'd forgotten how to use his legs, or a doctor had lied to him he couldn't, —acted in their house, though, his idle walking constituted part of instructions given him by his father, —once he arrived DonkeyVille Center: for his presence to be felt, —to parade himself in every which direction in front of their dome.

Yuug Behuul's presence saved proceedings for everyone involved, for soon, procedures recommenced relieving terror stricken touts--- certain their opportunity at earning plenty of extra income illegally enlisted elders agreed to pay—was now on cue to slip away, —their efforts in better part of several hours they spent pleading with everyone to calm down had only engendered a more adamant inaction from impatient seniors, those hours spent giving assurances to enthused prospective young again's—protocols had just been put in place to prevent a reoccurrence, had fallen on deaf ears, —a failure that in more ways than one, nearly amounted to every single racketeering gangster's own unsuccessful thievery from gullible proprietors: —who, —being selfless as they were, hadn't charged a dime to any hopeful seniors—even if theirs was a miscalculation on commencement of business over how they'd earn trillions of dollars in revenues, but are now faced with real chances of watching ordinary thugs striving hard to earn fabulous amounts from a charitable endeavor they worked hard to see continue.

Miscalculations were noted to have originally been part of Brask team's scheme, when, —armed with certain statues of law, several governments including Washington DC, had interjected into Brask's NewLife's business operations for what they called: 'an in-depth analysis' of Redwood's unprecedented medical device: but were actually saying in their own little roundabout way: '*hey, we heard what all of you did last time*', ---all of you meaning; NewLife's Brask partners, as well as any of their cohorts yet to be identified. '—*did last time*', —no less meaning some laws of Netherlands they purportedly violated on suspicion of hiding a delinquent Jon Schilling now Robin Hegan authorities over there had since charged with not wanting to pay debts incurred in a bet.

Other impugnable government activities around NewLife's operations such as: incessant letters of interrogation hinting on suspected Brask's culpability, screamed: *'hadn't you?'* —or, *'---at least it's what we heard you did'*, —or, *'you think we don't know.'* A few of governments' letters, more or less telephone calls downright said to them just as deviously: *'If you do as we tell you, there's not going to be a problem for anyone of you, you hear? ---we got out eyes on you!'* —Softer more accommodating female voices in subsequent follow up calls to previous callers would then say: *'Do what you gotta do, we got your back.'* This second call 'er' was usually an affirmation one needed, to know what was amiss. This approach to solicitation was a constant indicator past victims of extortion by government agents, swore was nearly never far behind, —following being kept on hold for continuing telephone conversation, for ample time that preceding caller presupposes is enough to induce an understanding of consequences of:—in this case, NewLife's: Brask team's presumed illegal actions under review, to elapse once that initial threats had been issued, to allow themselves be subdued into cooperation.

However, after covertly testing some pods in numerous franchised centers of NewLife Corporation using several efficient methods a state government devised to determine transmogrifier's efficacy, or its procedure's value to society, or whether it was imperiled to soon become a miss affair, interested franchisers hoping to operate one or more centers received go-aheads required for operations by way of licenses, essentially absolving NewLife's bleary eyed Mr. Brask, little perturbed Yuug Behuul, plus a formerly saddened Duran Buckler, —all of whom--suddenly felt unsure of what actions to take next—following such great news, —became more joyful than any other in celebrating victory, hence proving themselves to be, ---to paraphrase how several of their sassy kin, —even themselves, saw it: a set of ignoramuses yet to reach mastery in guileful art of public deception over their machine's capableness or purported good it promised to bring all concerned, being their sole reason for wanting its proliferation, —though, neither men, nor their minor—Yuug Behuul, ever set out to deceive anyone regarding their claims transmogrifier's lent youth back to seniors. These good tidings from all three tiers of governmental authorities, caused them celebration without cease.

Presumed charges of involvement in a likely foolish criminal act, not only of, —first offering their services free of charge, ---it was deciphered years later, pertained to their perceived zeal in harboring what numerous news media afterwards termed 'European fugitives', ---without intimating appropriate US authorities, especially being aware numerous laws prohibited such action, accordingly, even mere vestibules of suspicion—then, earned them: NewLife's entrepreneurs, a denial from fulfillment of their goal to make large monetary gains from providing F.O.Y technologies, in exchange for escaping a decade each, in jail—minus Yuug Behuul himself whom it turned was eligible for time in a juvenile detention center according to Dutch laws were matters to ever to get out of hand in further investigations proving his culpability.

These nearly unfortunate proprietors started out thinking, —not pennies, not dimes, but tons of dollars—they'd make from their endeavor earnings from constant flow of income accruing from efforts put into their investment in over a hundred franchised centers, but at long last, timely favorable decision by squared good fellows in Washington, —it was no use frustrating good country men out to do just service to mankind, otherwise, all there were to be gained for them would have been public hero statuses accompanied by handshakes.

Were these Brask's not already people of means, their operations inclination towards earning them zeros financially given government's unwelcome interjection into NewLife's affairs with even flimsy excuses, was set to become their life's sad story. Even dimes resulting from distributing earth's most important product after electricity – or, to befall man since his creation, —a product reported in legends centuries

later, to have settled humanity into a joyful expectation of longevity, or of permanent youth, ---if going by assurances —young Yuug Behuul—it's creator: a boy not quite ten, Mr. Brask in his forties: his father, as well as their octogenarian investor—it was said then, reverted to his mid-twenties---depending on what twists was contained in transmogrifier's legend apprised, —for he was still an eighty-five year old man, gave everyone people could last tens of thousands of years, was going to elude them.

Their assurances of clocking nine hundred-ninety-nine, plus another one year — to make it a thousand years of living---young again's could then multiplied by thirty, forty, even fifty times, ---elongating their lifetime to upwards of fifty thousand years, became another matter two government tiers: that of thirty states on one tier, in conjunction with Washington DC, tallied against NewLife enterprises, or their franchises, for one simple reason everyone else—not just qualified seniors, derived hopes from it, therefore, any eventualities coming short of expectations now, or later on, was going to equal a fraudulent declaration to entice unsuspecting publics, particularly earth's aging or aged masses everywhere.

Near exoticness of elderly folks who until recently were out of sorts with contemporary times, created a harmonic atmosphere everywhere they turned up, theirs became a unique partnership with society, people turned their heads to stare at sights of spell binding wonders a child's handwork evolved humans into once through with a product humankind hadn't seen coming, —or were doomed to still be hoping for—much as they'd since been hoping for it from time's onset, were Yuug Behuul's fountain of youth still only an imagination in his heart, or not come to man's timely aid; ---a precocious possibility medieval chemists, —to ones all through passing centuries of scientific advancements in their pursuit of knowledge of methods to develop longevity or retain youth even for a day longer, to those in present day pharmaceuticals all continually claiming was under development in one form or another; pills, lotions, magic potions, rubs, even incantations expected to render magical results of making patrons look, feel, if not be younger, in their establishments, but in truth has since, —irrespective of how much dexterity in science they possessed, remained mere fantasies in minds of such great chemists: Archimedes for one, others being; Darwin, Avon cosmetics, Roech pharmaceuticals, et, cetera, but which science or some clever corporation, or scientist has suddenly chanced upon in recent times, —resolutely cracking it wide open, still lacked in certain places requiring critical transmorgrifier influx given its necessitous nature.

It was somewhat gratifying to Yuug Behuul's team, —not his young gang—whose celebrity status had since depleted somewhat, but his corporate team, —to observe how those beneficiaries most advanced in years: centurions, nonagenarians, octogenarians, plus many—it must be said, were still in their fifties, ---though, a few instances of forty year old fellows—nostalgic over their twenties' era lifestyles angrily demand-

ing to be allowed to put themselves through transmogrification, —
began to struggle to adjust themselves into being an integral part of
modern traditions, lifestyles they thought they'd left behind a while
back, it increasingly became hopes in far younger country men they met
once back from senescence to begin leading a contended way of life far
better than what existed during their other youth.

Yuug Behuul's procedure brought humankind a great deal of
satisfaction, it was to a very great extent, reassuring to see smiles on
people's faces again. People formulated habits of peering closer at
everyone else, or casting second glances at other people, ---if only to
ascertain whether a person was an; 'actual young', a 'youngering fellow',
or a 'young again', a unanimous christenings by societies all over once
their eagerness to involve themselves in activities attributable to twenties, or thirties odd years old was perceived. It gradually became their
own way of testing out limits of their new circumstances, .

Many took to games of yesteryears; paragliding, or ski-jumping,
some enjoyed hiking, while others re-embraced boating. For others,
partaking in public event where over enthusiasm manifested itself in
incremental jubilatory shrieks at various points during events, was all
they needed to make them more wholesome—or so—they believed.
Others chose to maintain perfect solitude they'd always known to be
never far from their lives. One it was said, registered himself a member
of US Olympic team for a fifth attempt at capturing gold in a sport
providence had previously given him four opportunities in his younger
days, finishing last each time, —hoping Yuug Behuul would be there at
track side to cheer him on.

From news commentaries, a fairly disappointed Yuug Behuul
observed commentators he thought should have been proud of efforts
made by NewLife thus far to reach forward to congratulate him in every
word they spoke, instead, made annoying remarks suggesting an enduring lack of his device's proliferation wasn't entirely owing to prohibitive
cost of building each unit rumored to be a trillion dollars, or upwards
of two, but was due to unbridled laziness of it's makers.

For his age, Yuug Behuul's mental capacity could not fathom how a unit of anything could be dear enough to warrant not just one, but over one trillion dollars it costs of building just a unit of it, ---or where anyone wealthy enough to make such a costly expenditure to build one at a trillion or more dollars could be found, let alone agree to undertake underwriting costs for hundreds of units now installed in over one hundred centers all over America, in addition to a further two hundred units required to satisfy demands elsewhere around earth.

Some postulated rationales regarding its extra ordinary sumptuousness, was that a contrivance capable of achieving results as precious as what transmogrifiers installed in centers proudly displayed on TV screens during news hours by networks—viewers could never get enough of, was said to be constantly putting out, deserved to cost whatever unholy price was attributed to it.

However, opinions others ascribed to about its presumed scarcity was due to shipping costs---not of it's manufacturing, but generally, consensus despite every opposing argument, was: a government, or governments willing to ensure access to fountain of youths for its teeming elderly masses, was free of charge, should at least have ensured it was made more available. Others would however speculated over scarcities of building material in each pod known to emit strange sorts of hum---it was said NASA once stated was not to be found anywhere on earth, was responsible for it's one trillion or more dollar's cost. Arguments would go on endlessly, prompting smarter ones amongst excited news-mongers, or young again's to wonder, '—*where then did it come from?*'

14

*What good would new young's do
with a second youth.*

*I*n recent times, countless seniors desperate to maintain a society
of folks in their peerage for relations, visited government offices
numerous times to lobby stiff necked bureaucrats, demanding more---if
not everyone of their peers, be processed mandatorily to facilitate a
wholesomeness of their eldersome generation going forward youthful-
ly---taking stock of humankind's reluctance in accepting a thing called
fountain of youth existed even as it continued constantly engendered
welcomes for young again's in enthusiastic contemporaries of their
grand children waving white handkerchiefs at them where ever a recog-
nizable one was spotted.

There was joy, joy---in street corners, gatherings, malls, events, ---everywhere one looked, no one could foretell what era a final abatement of celebrations would occur, ---not that anyone wanted it to.

Somewhere in a public place reserved for meetings, faux Mr. Brask---by him their small one---but on special permission from chief Mr. Brask, stood observing events. In compliance with a stern cautionary word earlier on not to remove either his hat or his dark sunglasses he was instructed to put on to enhance his disguise of being someone else, ---as giving away identities was not part of their itinerary for any of their planned days event.

Yuug Behuul stood quietly, keenly observing every little going's-on as they occur, failing in that process to notice a man almost sneak up to them from areas behind where he stood with his guardian, to beseech them an indulgence of some of their time for a conversation.

Unaware he was about engaging whom newspapers famously tagged prominent Mr. Brask—NewLife's main driving force behind boosting transmogrifiers rapid distribution to diverse localities in America, —himself uncertain why, of all places—it was there he should find himself, other than to observe unending exhilaration in seniors unsuitably deemed young, whilst knowing such presumptions were wrong. After acknowledging greetings, they turned towards each other to engage themselves in a conversation from which each man hoped to extract or extrapolate certain information constantly elusive to him, or they'd find useful later on.

"These people—" said their new companion referring to over a hundred new young's milling around unassumingly, "---they exude contentment, or are often too overjoyed with turn of events in their lives, I mean over their new personalities---"

"You don't say---" agreed Mr. Brask—thought of---in all their new companion's presumptuousness was approximately his own age.

"Hello there," greeted Mr. Brask's new acquaintance to Yuggy, "—how may I refer to our young fellow here, is he a son of yours?" —inquired their new friend stretching his towards Yuug Behuul for a hand shake,

"Sorry, excuse my indifference, my young friend here is Y.G. Bighull, a cousin of mine, they are shipbuilders in his family, their vessels transport folks back to an earlier location, —should you or your folks ever need to travel back whence you started out, he's who you need to have on your side. Their new friend both Brask's noted didn't seem very much like one capable of buying even a conjectural vessel referenced moments ago, but then again, one never knew, —nodded his head just before taking Yuggy's hand in a firm hand shake,

"How are you today?" Asked their new mate,

"I'm OK," replied young Mr. Bighull wondering what other names remained for him to assume in this morning's prevailing order of silence before his work day's events elapsed,

"Glad, —I'm glad to hear it," said he quickly returning his attention to elder Mr. Brask moments before he said,

"You were making remarks about these young again's, weren't you—Mr. Bighull? —I assume that is your name as well—"

Borrowing a leaf from their new companion's train of thoughts, Duran Buckler began,

"Of course, like I was going to say, ---they sometimes suddenly burst into boisterous laughter——even when they're alone, though more boisterousness occur---I have noticed, —when there are a lot of them gathering. I also noticed how each relishes new found expectation of more life ahead of them, —like a prisoner looking forward to his liberty whilst heading home soon after getting out of jail, —what I find craziest about it all is—" said he in a furtherance to his yarn, "—sometimes, it is hard to tell them apart from us."

"I see---" replied his octogenarian countryman he still evidently assumed a peer, "---others welcomed them too I might add---" he added then turned Yuug Behuul whom it seemed was budding to make a comment, to signal his silence. In understanding, Yuug Behuul nodded his agreement.

"I understand there are---" began their new pal—who was so confident both Bighull's attention were his to finesse with —it no longer mattered introducing himself by name, "---there were three of them behind it; one everyone calls 'Mr. Brask', I understand he owns where transmogrifier now making waves was invented, or introduced to earth by its creators in Big Sur—California, —essentially---I understand, it was put in his care, he assumed ownership. . .",

"Really?" —sounded Mr. Bighull, feigning an undivided attention,

"Right, but can't really say, no one knows what's true anymore---" came a quick reply from a thrilled stranger his audience's attention was undivided, he continued, "---although Mr Brask—it was said, was known to have released news to media houses not long ago it belonged to his young son---you know? ---that little kid often seen at press conferences, or on news clips parading in front a tall glasslike shell—I believe that's what a transmogrifier is—" he was interrupted,

"Yes, ---yes---I remember seeing him once on TV," agreed attentive Mr. Bighull, "---ah! --that young fella! ---but how could that be? —such a thing is consequential on a small child's hard work?"

Ignoring his question, their talebearer friend continued,

"Well, if smarty-pants is it's actual owner, should it not be identified as his? ---mm? ---though I must admit it is a dad's duty to ensure it's keep or eventual distribution—till his boy is of age, hence must have now come to think himself as it's interim owner, ---besides, we also understand his father or some relative has since undergone transmogrification to boost his knowledge of their invention's work-ings to an in-depth one before making it public. I think they said that to achieve this, ---whoever that relative was—permitted a reversal of

himself back to youth in it without first it's workings or risks associated with it, to acquire first hand experience—if he were to gain just enough confidence from results of his own procedure to both make it known to all it was true, or that it existed."

"Wonderful!---" Suggested Bighull, "---tell me more." He was thrilled to hear about himself in what he apprised was now quickly transforming into a legend of how it was a certain second Mr. Brask, a once elderly man of eighty-seven, ---still was, ---whether it was apparent to anyone or not; ——after seriously considering many hardships he once endured during earlier times in his life, wisely decided to avoid such ever reoccurring—or to at least settle scores with fate, cleverly entered into an agreement with a family another acquaintance of his informed him was called 'Brask's, ——his namesake, to; firstly, permit him an early unqualified procedure to verify its authenticity, secondly, to allow him purport himself a relative of their's—permitted use of, or even combinations of every little designations with which their little son was identified: Morsan Brask, this it was said he opined was for a good purpose.

A startled Duran Buckler learned from this strange rumormonger—how venturesome Brask: he Duran Buckler, saw it an easy opportunity to utilize his own business acumen in first promoting a new spectrum of business, ——making every one of them rich, ——himself wealthier — but whilst still keeping it's ownership theirs, his identity secret ——should in case anything went wrong. He pointed out to them—it was also said, that bearing 'Morsan Brask' as his name bore many potentials to convince everyone it was Yuug Behuul's or his family, not any other behind its eventual proliferation.

Loud quibbling's on how strange it was for an unrelated namesake to even suggest to another family there was a good purpose of hoping to protect them—all associated with his usage of their name: so—should matters go awry, probabilities of law enforcement agents or agencies arresting 'Morsan Brask'---a minor child not prosecutable by law—therefore couldn't be held accountable in situations where such should have obtained, was reduced, endured all over.

Duran Buckler further stunned by strange accounts a totally unfamiliar person was giving about his exploits listened on almost too afraid to cut him short. He learned from further accounts, it was he—for his apparent slyness—everyone advised of his strategy suggested should occupy premiere position of blame, or sole ownership of, —not their budding corporation, but of general liabilities should failure or disappointment, if perhaps injuries occur.

Talebearer went on,

"We also learned this particular fellow, —it is conjectured is also called 'Duran Buckler' ---a billionaire from childhood---controlling or manipulating everyone for NewLife Corporation in such a conniving way should progress go south, it would be his namesakes: father—son team who should suffer consequences of facing investigations, not he, a mere investor."

"Oh---my!" Duran Buckler exclaimed, "---what everyone in America knows!" —thought he aloud,

"Indeed," agreed their acquaintance, "---everybody but he knows it," —he went on, "—people, ---meaning, —us in media organizations, also came to judgment it was manifestly evident his position was; if conversely, every billed procedure were accomplished everywhere uneventfully, all processed elders emerging all right, —thereby encouraging countless more potential beneficiaries to line up for a purchase of youth inducing procedure—wilfully turning in their cash to make them all rich, he, Duran Buckler---never a Morsan Brask—even richer, he could thereafter emerge as his real self, a 'Duran Buckler' he truly was, to take his rightful place amongst America's legendary folks.

"I see, I see!" Mr. Bighull said,

"But it wasn't to be, both he---Mr. Buckler, nor anyone else involved, could ever make any money now," he was told, "—as it might yet be banned due to certain other unethical practices."

"Why?" —he was asked abruptly,

"We heard they broke certain laws, one can't tell which exactly, ---but we'll see..."

Making no attempts to disguise what denoted a rude reminder of reality to his audience, this rumor monger to whom Duran Buckler suddenly took to disliking, cued on how due to no errors or mistakes by deserving communities, what amounted to humankind's centerpiece now stood on shaky foundation. Moments later, he witnessed his two listeners walk away from him with a lessened vitality than what he noticed about their persona when he first met them some minutes ago, without so much as a goodbye, apparently they cared little about any more of his accounts.

Later-on at dusk, all Brask men team sat around dinner table discussing matters over mouthfuls. Etiquette shoved aside, these men began dealing verbally with each other, they hashed over how their creation---which all three knew it wasn't, ---was impacting not only societies to which it would bring about change, but also, what efforts they needed making to reap rewards.

"Indeed," began Mr. Brask tapping a small trasnmogrifier model reported to be doing brisk business in department stores due to incessant pleas kids were entering everywhere before their parents to purchase one sometimes more, as toys, or keepsakes, —standing beside his bowl of cereals, "---all what your friend said to you near Laguna beach events earlier on, ---give or take a few tit bits, sounds like strategy---Mr. Buckler, a very good one if you ask me,"

"Perhaps not, Mr Brask, I too have good intentions—-you know? —it is saddening how a preemptive action by Washington —we couldn't see coming, outwitted us all," ---countered his now friendly investor, noting his hosts remarks somewhat uncannily resembled a blame on him, "—I think it's what he was aiming at saying this morn-ing."

"Still, ---dad, our operations should continue out of here in our house, because, following government's compilation of a list of old people it wanted favored downstairs in Jane's office ---" Yuug Behuul was saying, "I don't think they want us out of business—-I saw their list of seniors they have for us to make young again," but his father interrupted,

"---I see what you mean. Amongst them being favored first, ---Yuugy", he told his boy, "---are retired or long serving government employees, public servants with reputation of good service to country: generals, admirals, several presidents, ---including one peanuts made fortunate, ---we need not mention names,"

"But why dad, why is it we can't just help all old people without them interfering?" asked Yuug Behuul whom it appeared was overwhelmed by passion to get things going, or for such interferences by government.

"Son, authority's main reason---we're told, for authorizing their list---in what I think is a detour in their own initiative towards us, was to encourage beginnings of a reconstruction of elderly societies in our country to what legend, or picture books suggested it was decades ago; from fun underneath sunny skies, to flowery dresses, newly young fellows walking briskly but happily to jobs their entire lives revolved around---clad in dark suits, by permitting those on their list to be made young again---as a start in their strategy" explained Mr. Brask,

"But why?" ——inquired Yuugy still unable to understand, but wanting to,

"Yuggy, listen to what your father is trying to tell you, their main reason is to simulate certain gaieties of their era, it shouldn't be puzzling to anyone, I might add, if young again's eventually show reluctance in accepting present norms—as they return, I couldn't image such possibilities" said Mr. Buckler, "---people always adjust to their new environments no matter what it is," he added, "——moreover, it's also government's own way of creating awareness or verifying your transmogrifier's or existence."

This last remarks by Duran Buckler Yuug Behuul understood mattered a lot, he liked it tremendously, soon, his stuff could receive its final approval lacking any of government's remaining restrictions.

"Smarty pants they are, look how famous they made us, everybody now wants to be my friend in school" enjoined Yuug Behuul going back to his dinner, but only after proudly informing his small audience kids in his class competed over buying him ice cream or cookies since bursting into limelight, his tone of finality making both men howl in laughter,

"I think what your boy is trying to say is, ---it has boosted our morals too you know? ---being rejuvenation's sole proprietors, perhaps, those of franchisers in centers too, I think it represented government's own way of authenticating our machine, it means we're good in their eyes." Mr. Buckler explained. Yuug Behuul's father nodded his consent, it was an opinion he could go with, it couldn't be anything else. His presumption young elders population---which to all intents had compelled authorities to act, was a sizeable one, proved demonstrably true, ---virtually a quarter of America's population. To them, a materialization of more decadence than anyone of them could possibly bring to words, or have imagined in their time that now pervades nearly every facet of society anywhere one looked---needed tackling, moreover, present generations---he was certain, was being hell bent on holding fast to their own dogmatizing beliefs, hence misguided government's wanted them back to help return norms to what it presumes was once prevalent or is acceptable.

Mr. Brask recounted a recent event at a California center---it's owners infamously chose to install in a derelict building, several elders celebrated with hard spirits even before it was there turn in queue to go inside. Of course, outcomes were virtually guaranteed now---they believed, it was almost certainly going to be what others had enjoyed, so downed glass after glass of gin or whiskey, maybe rum, in continuing celebration in advance of a second youth they were about to catch, when they were rudely reminded by a twenty something year old, smarting due to his inability to obtain permission or find any excuses to join in on elderly people's liquor spree---someone invited him to bring his grandfather to see what could be done to help revert him to youth---after pitying his family for steady trepidations felt in anticipation of their grandfather's demise; how---whatever yesteryears represented for them, couldn't possibly compare to what modernistic people had going for them, nor could it equate what future times foreboded once they'd exited transmogrifier made available by modern contemporaries, therefore should not party like theirs was a better time. When challenged by alarmed fellows why he chose to address needy elders in such ungentlemanly manner,

"It is only when armed with knowledge of past errors, an option to attempt to rectify them to allow for a better tomorrow comes into existence, these dudes aren't back with any good motives—other than to take over our lives, party like they're doing right now, perhaps spoil everything some more." —jealousy had compelled him to retort.

Mr. Brask along with his associates: these two at table with him, —who had been in attendance all morning that day to help supervise proceedings, was was forced to lend his partial agreement, or support to an obviously annoyed young fellow where he stood by his grandfather, but was neither surprised to see it encouraged little conversation, nor would he take any action to try quelling further arrogance in whom thought it was due him.

"Theirs were oodles of errors in their time, errors too numerous to count," he suggested with an unusually raised voice to ensure others heard him,

Smiling with air of satisfaction, Duran Buckler put down his cutlery to make his opinion known,

"Still, we look upon new young's with admiration in our eyes, almost secretly wishing to one day be in their shoes,"

Mr. Brask, —vocally paraphrasing implications by his guest who's bearing until recently leaned heavily towards life's own far end, but was young again himself---a transformation he'd personally witnessed, though now—with regards to this argument, —holding onto an opposing viewpoint apropos which era owned a better epoch, suggesting what societies generally perceived of them since commencement of transmogrification to make elders wholesome again, hinted at how decadence, nonchalance, corruption, even unwarranted chaos, or their allowance of unwanted influx of people of other kinds coming in with with malign agendas or destructive traditions of other places in their hearts, —none in their time could prove existed—before encountering it, badly comprised future generations now in existence. Mr. Brask understood his son's ignorance over his last remarks, his son's young mind was too inexperienced to understand, ---all of these vices, or associated ills young again's currently frowned at their return, —which were some of many contributing factors to downfalls of past genera-tions, had also contributed to woes born by all today.

To drive home his point, he arched himself over towards Yuug Behuul to whisper,

"What they are trying to say-Yuugy, is, ---there could not possibly be a way future generation elderly folks are converging to join, could possibly equate unruffled tranquility or utter repose of their time---which although could not be exclusive of laziness, with success, because then, people thought well of each other or treated fellows well, ---a tradition now lost to antiquity. In those days, folks carried in their hearts---a uniform thought for societies own good when this country contained only just country folks. In some ways, we've managed to decipher from their attitudes they too entertained reservations about their predecessors like we do of them. However, their distastes hints on a want for a secure future now they were returning back to their youths again—in droves, they seem willing to participate, or are prepared to embrace hard work for former ideal to be restored succeeding eras."

"I thought so too dad," agreed Yuugy, but Mr. Brask just couldn't see such possibilities of his young son's growing mind possess-ing enough muster to grapple with arcane information inherent in his insinuation even he barely understood. He wouldn't understand either why old folks supposed they could provide successes posterity required for societies to be adjudged proper, when it was their failure, impedi-ments during their reign—this faltering era that constituted a future for them then currently suffers, emanated from their own unpreparedness or general apathy —while their generation manned every affair of our

country. Mr. Brask turned to Yuugy to offer a word of advice,
"Don't worry son, one day, you'll understand."

Equipped with empirical evidence Yuug Behuul of Wyoming's Brask
family's youth giving contrivance provided planet earth, —was safer
than many at highest levels of authority could ever wish it to be, —for
them to still be able to push their weight around—mandating boosting
of efforts through their orders, governments heaved sighs of relief, thus,
invigorated by so wonderful a progress, authorities eagerly continued
with enlisting more patients to such extents—Yuug Behuul's transmogrifier could almost have been theirs. As was it when government's began
investigations with tentative lists of risk takers, many to grace later lists
included great unsung government scientists whom nobody ever heard
of, — that generally, —for being without peer or rivals commanded
largest in class salaries, ---were abashed over such successful scientific
equipment reaching humans from another source other than their well
equipped laboratories, ---a situation good enough to cause early re-
trenchments, or hasty career changes should they ever learn a child bore
sole responsibility of transmogrifier's provision to humankind.

15

Peeled eyes are

Set for many tomorrows.

At long last, Yuug Behuul's dome shaped trasnmogrifier or, regres-sifier, —thought to be multiple times better than it's cousin, both came to gain acceptance from humanity, it's owner, proprietor's or investor's aspirations to earn fortunes from operating either twain rejuvenation utensils, broadened. They saw a silver lining in their effort, when authorities reached them with great news their counterparts in foreign lands wanted into America's youth capturing frenzy. Their interest in accepting units, or even one of a transmogrifier—were one all that could be spared, —not regressifier, since it might yet be farfetched to ask for that, to commence immediate resuscitation of their elderly population back to more vigorous activity, was well received, —however, for NewLife corp, or B .R .Ctr .Corp, such non-indigenous requests

warranted hefty price tags for overseas beneficiaries it was supposed numbered into a billion or two throughout earth, no one showed any surprise other sovereign lands all agreed to certain unfavorable terms, or conditions associated with it offered them.

NewLife's owners learned forthwith, —that greedy bureaucrats in all three tiers of government's—too, wanted a percentage per person of any foreign income to enable them better facilitate international transactions for mounting numbers of customers assigned to domes a citizen of their state or country registered in those countries, —to which NewLife's proprietors hardly believing their good fortune, eagerly agreed, —though still cursed their luck for starting a business venture set to make many who never worked a moment to ensure it's availability, rich.

Everywhere one looked, there was more chaos over becoming young again than one could possibly bring to words, fist raising angry people—whose youthfulness effectively excluded from eligibility to undergo transmogrification, dotted towns, cities chanting; *Yuggy, Yuggy,* —offering adjurations to either utensil's young inventor—in addition to their agitation for production of more pods to satisfy an ever-increasing demand for youth, they were also seizing any requisite opportunity to try their hands at canvassing for spots—if not at Big Sur mansion—a place agreeably beyond their reach, then, at any restorals center nearest their homes, for aging or elderly folks in their families.

Multitudes could be seen lined up in front of TV cameras threatening vengeance except given privileges of catching a glimpse of Yuggy's behemoth---it was said, still loomed with its calm ominous ambience in a corner of his family's Big Sur mansion.

Shoving what remained of media house's egos aside, executives galvanized a constant flow of people to serve them purposes of, —not just being their front—nor only being medium through which their networks reached Redwood—even if only in spirit, but also to represent popular demands of ensuring a wider distribution of a child's life altering gizmo by permitting correspondence to pour into their stations through angry letters, faxes, emails filled with threats, irate telephone calls, but in all, these joyful unrests were also about encouraging hopes for everyone seeking opportunity to visit iconic Redwood mansion harboring an equally iconic presence of mysterious eight story high dome thought to exude holiness—but lived far away, by providing just a moment's exposure on their networks, to see if earning themselves good ratings like never before was a possibility.

Yuug Behuul's celebrity status grew rapidly, almost keeping pace with Redwood's peculiar enterprise he, his father along with their friend Billionaire Buckler ran. Home schooling proved a better option to pave way for posing before news crews from various networks, in some cases private media houses perpetually asking to make appointments for paid photo sessions with Yuug Behuul.

Other private establishment's boards of director's---though issued large sums purportedly to fund his consent for studios to capture his images, then always keeping more than ninety percent change left for themselves: fraud, it's cousin embezzlement never ceasing to be part of their calculations. Independent photo journalists seeking a break, would merely turn up to in Jove's name solicit, —sometimes a little too forcefully, —his photos, for what they claimed was a good services for societies all over craving knowledge of his person even it be only in photographs. Smart phone selfies with fans beaming with smiles became a mainstay of his day as well.

Wealthy elders long done with their wills regarding whom of their children they wished to favor with their fortunes, corporations, estates, investments, live's savings, properties, once again revisited it, wept a little, but there now being real chances of recovery from senility, hired attorneys, there wasn't any person alive at this point ignorant of what capabilities earth's most wondrous invention they heard a kid crafted to aptly harness its capabilities in making folks like them young again.

A lot of seniors long concluded with plans to hand their wills over to their lawyers were forced to keep it's contents away from any knowledge of inquisitive relatives more-so children or their lawyers themselves---claiming some 'foundation', ---which in most cases were none existent, —but was merely being interposed into conversations or arguments to keep covetous kin wary of enabling their quicker demise to expedite succession to any available patrimony. There was a common approach amongst rich old folks of employing obstinacy as their only strategy to clinging onto several aspects of their beings, ---particularly their worth first, then their lives, if finally, a resolution of fears of their condition known to be unremittingly surrounded on all corners; front, back, left as well as—at it's right side---in corresponding order by, illnesses, anxieties, remorse over; what remained unaccomplished, regret over opportunities lost, —at both ends of it's vertical bearing; by fear of one's imminent demise, then, —elderly folks constant thought of how fast time flew by, is at long last provided by a ten year old Yuug Behuul reliable sources say was now a celebrity circumstances brought into limelight that morning he was first spotted by viewers at home on a west coast TV show showcasing his life altering gizmo.

He was a few inches taller now, all bubbly all smart, ever present in his country men's prayers, or thoughts of seniors everywhere. These days, he is seen about in fancy suits, tall bowler hats thought to make him look more mature. He carries with him at all times, a demeanor of importance, an advice from his best buddies to which he clung earnestly.

When last anyone heard of him before retiring to rest till another interview, was a recent evening when in what was a coached session of how he could shed more light on his dome's safety---following numerous procedures of his elderly friends, his trusted associates, but most importantly, his own grandmother---government records show along with others, was truly a beneficiary of his transmogrifier's life altering scientific capabilities, —which he corroborated that day when informed throngs at a TV studio session in no uncertain words, was that young twenty year old girl seen in transmogrifier's TV commercial. This news caused Yuug Behuul's young face to permanently light up with a smile,

"Oh—my!" —said he to an interrogating journalist, what bothered him most wasn't when he'd ever get to have another chance to go back to being a kid again, '---how he just itched so badly for when his turn for transmogrification finally arrives in his old age, but till then, —considering many centuries his trasnmogrifier promises, ---in many obscure cases---is already known appended to human life, a hundred years---when humans gifted with longevity are ultimately betrayed by it---is now tantamount to early eras of one's life.

Finally, humankind's comprehension—it was Most High's providence of a life altering technology to humanity—following what they would realize later, was through Yuug Behuul's unrelenting diligent work for him, longevity of hundreds of centuries beyond what obtains now---as well as many unrevealed privileges, is now bestowed on humanity; no longer would anyone's journey on earth fade too soon leaving countless many devoid of fulfillment, an era, —whereupon no senior, or elder, no citizen, no countryman or woman should ever again die during dawn of one's life.

YUUG BEHUUL
AND THE
FOUNTAIN OF YOUTH:

---tells a story of a young child: Morsan Brask, known by many as Yuug Behuul, was suddenly thrust into limelight when his technology solves age old questions of youth and longevity.

Soon after he realizes a transmogrifier in his home brought to him by higher beings could reverse seniors to youngsters, aged to minors, senile to youthful, adding thousands of years to human life, government's around earth and people's from everywhere come calling with various extra ordinary strategies to take advantage of his machine or get involved for whatever gains could be made.

Bets lost turn out to be wins for certain individuals as aged folks in societies all over begin reverting to earlier stages in their lives, bringing with them promises to make good on their past errors on society with their second youth as they begin anew.

With unfolding events arrive fame to rob little Yuugy of his childhood as he constantly addresses humanity through world's media's not to worry about a thing as life has only just begun.

ABOUT THE AUTHOR

Don M Denn is a nature enthusiast and an educator from Wyoming. While living abroad, he gained meaningful knowledge about various foreign cultures and traditions. In his free time he builds radio control scale trucks and competition Crawlers, loves music making. Don M Denn is a technology developer of an extraordinary sort.

He writes novels, poetry collections and novellas with various other pen names. He lives in the USA.

Printed in Great Britain
by Amazon

78488524R00108